# Echoes of Creation

## From the Echoes of History

### By Lance Conrad

To Lucas,

DawnStar
PRESS

The following is a work of fiction. All names, places, characters
and events portrayed herein are the invention of the author's
imagination or are used fictitiously. Any similarity to any real
persons or occurrences is purely coincidental.

Echoes of Creation

For information about discounts, bulk purchases, or reproduction
of content in this book, please contact Dawn Star Press:

info@dawnstarpress.com

ISBN: 978-1-7333406-0-1

Printed in the United States of America

Dedicated to my brother Wil.
I remember your miracle.

# Chapter 1

Sadavir rolled out of a deep sleep into a ready crouch in one fluid motion. He listened to the night, but everything was silent. He didn't move, using the darkness as a hiding place. He had always felt very comfortable in the dark.

Still, he had no idea what he was listening for. Something had woken him up and he could sense, more than feel, the faint ripples of darkness on the surface of his Stone. His Stone only activated when he was in danger.

It could mean that he had found what he was looking for.

*******

The past five years had been a booming time for the people of Surac. It had been rough in the beginning. The Creators and Destroyers had been separated for longer than anyone could remember. The fear and prejudices of generations didn't fade overnight. Still, it's hard to argue with success, especially success on such an astonishing scale.

The combined powers of the Stones had brought

both peoples an era of prosperity none of them could have imagined. The ability to shape the elements at will when a Creator and a Destroyer worked together had led to an abundance for anyone and everyone willing to step into this new paradigm.

There were limits to the power of the Stones. For instance, how well the power worked was incredibly dependent on the two people working together. Physical proximity, unity of purpose, and even personal connection between the two people all had drastic effects on how accurately and powerfully the Stones could be wielded.

For people who had spent their entire lives hating and fearing each other, there were many obstacles to a system that demanded deep cooperation. Luckily, there were examples to guide them. Leading the efforts were Aric, Sadavir's father, and Andre, the man who had taken Sadavir in when he had been banished to the land of the Destroyers five years earlier. The two men acted like long-lost brothers, working in unison from the beginning. Their dark blue Stones let them take their imaginings and turn them into solid metal. It wasn't long before other people were bringing new ideas for them to try out.

Aric had pouted for all of two days when the Destroyers had surpassed all of his cleverness in inventing. Their natural ingenuity had proven priceless and new machines and structures had been popping up all over the land, built perfectly and in shockingly little time, thanks to the constructive power of the Stones.

Used to being the smartest in the village before the Destroyers came, Aric now found that he had been a big fish in a little pond. Even the Destroyer children had been able to understand and even suggest improvements for his most advanced designs.

Still, the feeling of disappointment passed as soon as the Destroyers started bringing out their own designs. His boyish enthusiasm, so contagious and endearing, especially on a man of his immense bulk, had trumped all else and he spent most of his days talking over new ideas with Andre. By necessity, Aric's wife, Lauria, and Andre's wife, Nadya, had formed their own partnership. They didn't have the same color Stones, but they had their own form of power that usually accomplished more than the glowing light of the Stones: influence. The two women formed a bridge between the two peoples. Lauria was warm and caring, the type of person people hate to disappoint. Nadya was direct and forceful, the type of person people hate to anger.

Between the two of them, they managed to direct the efforts of their husbands towards useful and practical endeavors, and then work among the people to get them to adopt the new innovations.

If both gentle and direct methods failed, Lauria didn't mind invoking her son's name to nudge a holdout toward a more enlightened way of thinking. What Sadavir had done while bringing the people together had been nothing short of legendary. However, even the fantastical truth couldn't compare to how the story grew in the years after.

Oddly enough, it was the fighters and belligerents of both sides that tended to exaggerate Sadavir's abilities with each new telling of the story. At the end of the day, they couldn't deny that Sadavir had beaten them. And if given the choice, a proud man would much rather believe that it took someone legendary to beat them.

So while the original battle had been a team effort with Sadavir as the point of the spear, everyone now chose to remember it as Sadavir dominating all who opposed him.

The people now looked to him as a kind of figurehead leader. He didn't really pass or enforce laws, but everyone knew in their hearts that if Sadavir were to command something, they would obey. It was an amalgam of fear, respect, and awe.

Luckily, Sadavir had little interest in ruling, besides occasionally breaking up the fights that popped up here and there. So Lauria occasionally borrowed her son's implied authority to help ease the transition.

In the last year, a project had started that had seemed innocent at first, so Lauria and Nadya had decided to let the thing alone to succeed or wilt on its

4

own momentum. Some nameless Destroyer in a nearby settlement had invented a simple modular scaffolding. The design had spread and most people used it to build bigger houses.

Then, Vova, Sadavir's friend and music tutor, had suggested that the scaffolding could be used to scale the cliffs far to the north.

The cliffs had stood as an absolute barrier for all of their recorded history. Some monumental geologic force had sheared the land like a loaf of bread being torn in half, driving one land mass far above the other at a sharp angle.

If it had been softer stone, the cliffs would have degraded over time and maybe small pathways could have been discovered. As it was, the bedrock had been a granite that held its form remarkably well, so the towering cliffs remained impassable.

In this new age of power however, everything that had once been impossible was now being explored. Teams got together to build the structure. It was the largest single project the people had started on since the hated wall that had split their land for countless generations.

Skill and unity improved as two person teams worked to shape metal and rock. Strong iron molded into place by those with dark blue Stones. Then the rock itself was formed over the metal under the pale blue light that exerted power over the rock.

Day after day the scaffolding grew up the side

of the cliff like iron ivy. Construction slowed toward the end, as many of the teams quit, being too afraid of working on the heights. The workers had grown up on plains on the Creators' side of the wall and forest and hills on the Destroyers' side. Even the trees weren't especially tall. So no one had ever been this high off the ground before.

It was deeply unnerving.

Still, a few dauntless souls persevered until finally steel cleared stone and there was a passage that led to this highest land of their small continent.

Oddly, it had taken longer to gather explorers for the new land together than it had to build the scaffolding itself. The daily demands in their own places hadn't slowed, and many, especially among the Creators, did not understand why they should be sending good men off into the unknown to explore lands that hadn't ever mattered to them.

Still, Vova had taken ownership of the project and kept pressing until a couple teams had formed. Most of them had been Destroyers, but there were a few of the braver Creators who went along, mostly young men looking to prove themselves.

It was a common impulse among the young men now. Most Creators had grown up only doing light farm work and having plenty to eat. Now that the Destroyers roamed freely among them, many of the young Creator women took more than a second look at the tanned, toned, and rugged Destroyers.

Consequently, the Creator boys had taken a greater interest in the outdoors, trying more things and taking greater risks to stand out from the crowd.

So two exploring parties had climbed the scaffolding, parted ways at the top, and took off in opposing directions, agreeing to come back and report at the end of the week.

They were now three days late.

# Chapter 2

If only one party had been late, it might have been dismissed, but both parties being late had ignited paranoia in the people. This was completely new territory for them, after all. Who knew what dangers might be lurking?

The cry went up immediately for rescue parties. Unfortunately, very few answered the call. Those brave or foolhardy enough to make the attempt had been in the first parties. Now that those people had gone missing, few felt like venturing after them.

So only those personally tied to the missing explorers stepped forward, families and dear friends. However, love is no safe substitute for ability, and many of the willing crowd were too old, too young, or just too civilized to make the climb up the scaffolding and push into uncharted wilderness.

Still, they had been brave enough to gather a few supplies and come to Sadavir, offering themselves as rescuers.

Sadavir had scanned the assembled people with a heavy heart. There was no use in sending these willing souls after the lost people. It would only create three lost parties instead of two. The solution had been immediately clear. He told the people to go back to their homes.

He would go after the missing parties himself.

Most of the would-be heroes dispersed willingly, many of them with grateful tears in their eyes. Only a few stayed behind to offer their help. Sadavir denied them as well. He would go alone.

Without anyone else to watch over, he could move faster and farther. Also, if a threat had incapacitated the parties, he was the best suited to deal with it. And he fought best when he didn't have to worry about who else might be getting hurt.

There were light protests, but even those last few accepted Sadavir's decision and turned their feet toward home. Sadavir drew a deep sigh watching them go. He knew that they had been the easy ones to convince.

His next hurdle had presented itself immediately. Aric and Lauria pounced as soon as the last people had turned their backs. They informed their son that he simply wasn't allowed to go. It was too dangerous, people needed him, Olya needed him, and so on.

Sadavir knew his parents all too well and was ready with a single counterargument to match all of theirs.

"So we let them die? Who else do we send?"

Sadavir's life was defined and driven by a fierce

9

morality. As a small child, he had chosen to put his life on the line to protect the lives of others. This unbend-able standard had been taught, trained, and drilled into him by his parents. He now used it against them.

They still couldn't agree with his decision, but they also couldn't come up with any arguments that wouldn't be risking the lives of the lost explorers. So, they accepted their defeat and left the battle to the one with the worthiest claim: Olya, Sadavir's wife.

She, however, had already considered the risks and costs and had come up with her own solution.

She had put on her most determined face, the one that Sadavir knew he would be a fool to argue with. She sat him down and held his gaze for a full count of ten before speaking, just so he would know how serious she was.

"I'm coming with you." She laid all of her feminine will into it, her full force of personality. Such a perfect storm of conviction would win the day for her as it had so many times before.

Sadavir laughed, full and loud, a heritage from his father. Olya tried to keep on her brave face, to try and salvage the argument, but her perfect storm had no more force than a summer breeze.

She had tried her best, but couldn't blame her husband. Like his parents, she found herself at the mercy of her own prior argument. Naturally, Sadavir had wanted to go with the explorers in the first place.

He had hungered for the adventure. She had shut that down easily with the brutal efficiency of a single reason:

She was seven months pregnant with their first child.

At least, she thought it was just one child. The women of the village clucked and muttered every time they saw her belly. At seven months, she was already as big as most women were at nine. Rumors abounded about twins. Olya had blanched when she had seen one woman, talking to her husband and motioning towards Olya's belly, hold up three fingers.

That turgid belly that had held Sadavir close to home now held Olya just as fast. She also knew she couldn't ask him to let people die just for her. He might just do it.

Still, she still couldn't come to grips with him leaving. They did everything together. That's how it had to be. They complemented each other far more than just their Stones. Every weakness and strength of one was compensated for or enhanced by the abilities of the other. She couldn't imagine being away from him.

So she decided that she was offended at his laughter. She stood up and stormed off as best as she could.

She didn't plan any particular route, storming away doesn't work that way. Still, somehow, she found herself seeking out Lauria. Olya had been raised as an orphan, so Lauria was the closest thing she had to a mother. She found her leaving Nadya's house. Bloodshot eyes made it plain that she had been crying. Olya rushed to her and the two comforted each other a moment before Olya could speak.

"How can he go like this?" Olya demanded.

"I blame his father." Lauria quipped. The light joke softened Olya's anger and Lauria continued to share what consolation she had been able to find herself or borrow from Nadya.

"I had to watch him leave, too. People keep saying that he was banished, but I was there. He chose to leave himself. I knew why he was doing it, but it still hurt."

"It's good you had Aric." Olya offered, feeling an added measure of camaraderie with her mother-in-law. Lauria snorted.

"He wasn't much use. It's hard for a mother to admit that anyone could love her boy as much as she does, but I have to admit I never thought a father could be that devoted to his son. Sadavir leaving broke him up in a big way. Do you know where he was the whole night before Sadavir left?"

"Where?"

"Out in his shed, making Sadavir a new pair of armbands. Can you imagine how much I needed my husband that night? I was angry with him for a week after that."

12

In spite of the sadness of the story, Lauria smiled at the memory.

"Now that everything has passed, I understand why. Don't you ever tell him this, but he was right. I wanted to protect my child, to keep him safe. I did everything I could to keep the bad parts of the world away. Sometimes it even felt like I needed to protect Sadavir from Aric and his crazy training and inventions.

"It wasn't until later that I realized that Aric was also trying to protect Sadavir. The difference was that he protected our son by making him equal to anything the world could throw at him. When everything fell apart, my protection failed, Aric's succeeded."

"Do you think he can still protect him now?" Tears were in Olya's eyes. She was getting very near to the question her mind had been avoiding. Lauria made her face it.

"You mean do I think that Sadavir will make it back safe again." Lauria said it with the certainty of someone who was going down the same path. Olya nodded.

"Nadya just helped me with that, in her own way." Lauria began, nodding her head towards the closed door behind her. "She told me to list everything that I thought could kill Sadavir."

# Chapter 3

Olya gasped, more than a little outraged. Prompting a worried mother to picture ways that her son might die sounded outrageously cruel.

"That's horrible!"

Lauria nodded, but her eyes remained dry.

"I thought so as well, but you go ahead and try it."

"How..." Olya's tears, which had dried for a short moment of outrage, were now flowing as she faced the fear that haunted her. "There's so many! He could... What if he... Or..."

Lauria waited while Olya's terrified eyes flickered and she stammered through a list of thoughts, each one fizzling out before she could speak it. Finally, the torrent slowed and Olya's hands stopped shaking.

"Most of them aren't very realistic once you think about them directly." Lauria observed. "You know as well as I do that he can't be surprised, even when sleeping. There's nobody who can match him in any physical contest. His instincts were superb even before they were enhanced by his Stone. Do you imagine that he's going to trip and fall off a cliff?"

In spite of herself, Olya laughed. It was ludicrous to imagine Sadavir bumbling to his death.

"Did you come up with any?" Olya asked. It seemed less scary now to talk about it.

"Landslide." Lauria winked and the two women hugged again. "I'm as worried as you are, but if there's one force in this world that could plunge into the unknown and bring everyone back safely, it's our Sadavir."

That night, after a quiet dinner, Olya walked back to their room and emerged with a heavy wooden box. It was secured with an intricate iron lock, Aric's distinctive handiwork.

Olya wore the key around her neck like other women would wear jewels. She pulled it over her head and fitted it into the lock. It came free with an easy click and she lifted the lid. The steel armbands stared back at her from inside and she found she was crying again.

Sadavir hadn't worn them since that day, the day when the peoples had united. The day Uncle left. There had been little fights, of course, but Sadavir's natural abilities and his reputation had made them very short-lived skirmishes. There had been no looming danger that required the protection of the armbands. The armbands were only necessary if something had the potential to kill him.

Now that she saw them, she felt all the old fears

flood back at once. Somehow they were made even sharper for the fact that she hadn't needed to worry for so long.

Sadavir had sensed the moment of ceremony and offered her his arms, palms up. There was no use in telling her not to worry, or to assure her that everything would be fine. She was far too smart for that. If it had been an easy task, he would have sent someone else.

She pulled the first armband from the box, the one marked, "Honor." She grit her teeth, taking some small comfort in the feel of the cold steel. It was some of Aric's finest work. The power of the combined Stones could have made armbands in about a minute, but they would be crude things, solidly shaped, but lacking the master's touch.

Metal crafted by the Stones acted like new steel. Aric had taught her that steel needed to be stressed to become strong. There were hundreds of little secrets. The steel was heated, pounded, folded, and cooled, often many times over.

The process made the steel stronger, Aric had explained. As long as the steel was good, it would make it far more resilient than steel that had been smelted or crafted by the power of the Stones. Aric had glanced at Sadavir as he explained.

Olya had understood immediately. Aric's son was the steel, and he had put him through enough stress to strengthen and test him a hundred times

16

over. Lesser steel would have broken. Aric had confided in Olya that he had always expected there to come a point when Sadavir rebelled against him, or tried to quit his training. But the steel in the boy had come back stronger from every plunge into the fire, every stroke of the hammer, and every dousing in disappointment.

These thoughts flowed through Olya's mind like an elixir as she strapped the armband on to Sadavir's left arm. They reassured her, made her feel stronger. Sadavir was more than his training or his Stone. He was the good steel. Surely he might face terrible trouble on this excursion, but he would always bounce back. Wouldn't he?

Her courage grew even more as she reached for the second armband, the one marked "Love." She knew that, at the time, Aric had carved the word into the band to remind Sadavir that his parents loved him as he crossed over the wall. It had been meant to keep him from turning bitter at the injustice of his situation.

Now, the word brought to her mind the words of Uncle, spoken from the darkness on that darkest of nights for her. He told her about the voice that people in love hear, the one that tells them that their beloved can do anything. He had advised her to listen to that voice, even if it was foolish.

She listened now as she strapped the armband firmly in place on his right arm. Sadavir would be all right. She knew that because her heart simply couldn't imagine a world without him in it. Everything would be all right.

With all of these comforting thoughts buoying up her spirits, she couldn't quite understand why the armbands had so many of her tears on them.

# Chapter 4

Sadavir held completely still in the darkness, listening hard for whatever had awoken him. The night was unnaturally quiet and he strained to hear the soft whispers of motion that might indicate the presence of an attacker.

He yelped as his straining ears were assaulted by a piercing, trumpeting noise that shook the night with its resonance. He had never heard anything like it in his life. The awful sound was almost immediately followed by loud crashing that grew louder by the second.

Whatever was coming out of the darkness, it was big, sounded angry, and was coming right for him.

Resorting to tried and true tactics, Sadavir leapt into the tree by him, easily catching at a low branch even in the dark and pulling himself up into the branches. The crashing grew much worse and the tree started shaking as Sadavir clung to it.

What happened next was like a scene from a nightmare. A creature tore out of the darkness like a demon ripping itself free from the abyss. A torrent of mass and motion, the thing threw itself right at the tree Sadavir clung to.

He only had a moment to register the insane rage of the creature before he was scrambling through the branches, avoiding what looked like long claws in the dark. The thing was bigger than he had expected, bigger than he could have imagined.

After the first couple swipes missed, thanks to Sadavir's quick reflexes, the beast turned its rage on the tree itself. There was a momentary crunching noise as the long claws sunk into the tree, a moment of silence as enormous muscles tensed with unbelievable power, and then the tree was moving under Sadavir. It crashed down among the other trees, which managed to slow its fall a little, but also served to supply an entire legion of clubs as Sadavir was mashed between trees with nothing to do but hold on.

He gasped and gulped for breath as one branch caught him in the side. The pressure was unbelievable for one excruciating moment before the branch broke under the strain. The jagged wood of the broken branch hit Sadavir next, ripping a ragged gash in his side near the bottom of his rib cage.

Then he was on the ground, the tree a mess of branches pressing on top of him and the long claws reaching through after him. He moved instinctively, like a wild animal scrambling in the dark. His heels dug frantic furrows in the soil as he propelled himself

20

backward through the tangle, still on his back.

His Stone must have still been working on some level, because every claw that got near him clanged off his armbands, even though Sadavir himself had no real idea of where the strikes were coming from. The creature seemed to be everywhere.

Fueled by panic, Sadavir wrenched himself free of the crush of branches and hurtled through the dark, bouncing into trees and tripping over debris in his mad flight. He held one arm to his side and could feel the damage that had been done to him. Luckily, the shock of the experience and the adrenaline coursing through his veins kept him from feeling much pain.

But he knew that wouldn't last. The pain would hit him soon and it would limit his motion. He had suffered plenty of injuries during his training. He knew exactly how his body would react. Reflexes would slow and movements would stiffen as his body tried to protect the wounded area.

Worse, he was bleeding openly, he could feel it running down his side and onto his leg. He needed to rest and stop the bleeding right away. It certainly wouldn't be stopping on its own the way he was tripping and scrambling through the woods, the wound pulling at every jolt.

But he had to continue. In fact, his current efforts were painfully insufficient. There had been a small head start as the creature had not realized immediately that its quarry had escaped and it had continued to thrash at the tree for another minute before starting to chase after Sadavir.

But he could hear it now, making no effort to be quiet. If anything, it was tripping and running into trees as much as he was. The difference was that the creature didn't seem to be slowed down by the trees. The woody vegetation seemed only a minor obstacle as it thundered its way towards its prey, a relentless force.

Now it was getting closer. It would be on top of him in another minute and for the first time in his life, Sadavir felt truly helpless. He wasn't fast enough or strong enough to meet this challenge. He was the best trained fighter anyone had ever known or heard of, but he had been trained to fight people, not nightmare creatures.

Not good enough. The thought resonated like a death knell in his mind and for three full steps, he felt like giving up.

On the fourth step, he got angry. He had never given up on anything his entire life, and that was with everyone against him. Now he had the respect of two nations and a wife and family to go home to. Was he really going to choose this moment to lose his nerve?

The shame and anger worked like a shot of energy. His teeth set in a hard line and his nostrils flared as he tapped into something primal within himself. He would destroy this monster and anything else that stood between him and home, be it ten times as big.

The sudden surge of rage surprised him, even scared him a little. He had always fought from a sense of duty, and always with the least amount of force necessary. At this moment, he felt like dropping all such moral guidelines. He felt like destroying.

A part of his mind rebelled at the savagery, but even his logical side had to agree that the feelings were exactly what he needed to keep going under these conditions. So he embraced the inferno of emotions and bared his teeth to the night, a growl rumbling deep in his chest.

Luckily, even the savage part of his brain realized that speed and anger alone wouldn't be enough to defeat or even escape this creature. He'd have to be more than fast or strong. He needed to be smart. What would his father or Andre do?

What would Uncle Amar do?

Uncle Amar had never been afraid. Not when he was being held and threatened with knives, not when the entire village had wanted him gone or dead. He had always seemed to know more than everyone else, and that knowledge had given him confidence.

Sadavir tried to think like Uncle Amar now. What did he know? He knew he couldn't hide in a tree, that was for sure, he thought wryly. Then he stopped himself.

Why hadn't he been able to hide in a tree?

He had jumped into the tree long before the creature would have been able to see him. But the creature had come straight at him, had known exactly where he was without even checking other trees.

So the creature could see in the dark, he reasoned. He discarded the thought immediately, it being disproved by the cacophony that was nearly on top of him. If the creature could see in the dark, it wouldn't be tripping over every root and crashing into every tree like it was doing.

So how did it know his location? Had he made a sound? Something to give away his position? Sadavir knew it was possible, of course, but he couldn't quite make himself believe it. He knew how to move without making any sound.

Smell, it had to be smell. Unless the monster had some sort of extra ability that allowed it to sense him. Sadavir gulped at the idea. If that were true, and the monster had abilities beyond nature, like the Stones, then he might truly be at the end.

He shook the feeling away, he wouldn't despair again. So it had to be smell, he told himself. The creature had smelled him and had tracked him to his campsite and right into his tree.

# Chapter 5

Without slowing, Sadavir whipped his shirt over his head and wrapped it into a tight ball as he ran. He would only get one chance to test his theory. The creature was so close behind him now that Sadavir could hear a rhythmic scraping sound that must be a result of the creature's own movement. His back tingled, as if expecting a claw between his shoulder blades at any moment.

He held the balled shirt tightly in his right hand, feeling pleased for the first time that the shirt had so much blood on it. It would smell strongly like him. He whipped his arm back and brought it forward in a powerful throw, the shirt flying out in front of him.

At the same moment, he slammed his foot forward, digging his heel into the loamy forest floor, grinding to a sudden halt. He scrambled out of the way at a sharp angle, heading off in a new direction. It felt like the creature passed right by on his heels. Sadavir half expected the thing to stay right on top of him, but the beast tore right by.

Sadavir grit his teeth in grim satisfaction as he heard the beast thrashing around in the darkness upon finding his bloody shirt. It seemed confused, scratching at trees and clawing at the ground, presumably looking for him.

He was not so foolish as to believe that he had escaped. The thing would realize its mistake very soon and would be hot on his trail shortly. Sadavir knew he likely had less than a minute. More than enough time, he thought to himself, feeling powerful once more at having found an advantage over his enemy.

From all the falling and scrambling he had done, both knees on his pants had ripped. He used the rips now to tear off the lower legs on his pants. He now had two more decoys, one in each hand. As he ran, he used the rags to swipe blood from his side. He cringed in pain as one of the rags scraped across the wound.

The shock was already wearing off and the pain was building. He could feel his steady running rhythm starting to falter as his body tried to keep the wound from pulling open. That pulled his left side shorter and threw off his balance. He needed time, and lots of it, to take care of his wounds and think through the situation, more than he would gain from small distractions.

He heard the creature finally give up on his shirt and start heading his direction again. Sadavir threw one of his bloody rags straight forward again and turned, running straight back along his path. He was

26

running right towards the creature.

After he had covered a good distance, he turned sharply to the left and started running off at an angle. He could hear the creature coming closer now, moving faster now that it had caught onto his scent again. He threw his next rag forward again and turned straight back again, re-crossing his path.

He kept running straight on from there. The monster would likely continue on a straight line, reaching the end of the path and fumbling around for a while longer before it discovered he wasn't there anymore. Then it would head back along the trail. But this time it would find two branching scent trails. If Sadavir had any luck at all, it would follow the first one, heading toward the closer smell of blood on the cloth rag.

But even if not, Sadavir would have another significant head start. All he had to do now was to capitalize on it to buy himself a longer rest. He performed several more backtracks, using blood from his side to paint trees in false directions. Luckily his side had largely stopped bleeding now, though the pain was now becoming a major hindrance.

He had also lost enough blood that his head was feeling heavy and dizzy, as if he had been running all day, rather than the ten minutes that had actually passed. He heard a loud bellowing from the monster, a cry of frustration at losing its prey. The sound was distant and not getting any closer.

Sadavir felt little relief at this. He had managed to fool the creature, but it was only a matter of time before it crossed his trail again, his real trail. At least it might not be tonight, he told himself, trying to be optimistic.

After all, the creature had not shown a true hunter's determination. There was rage and savagery, but something that large was probably used to crushing its prey within the first couple moments. It wouldn't be built for a long chase. It was just too big for that kind of endurance, he told himself.

Sadavir's own muscles were feeling a little sluggish, but he was still feeling light mentally at his momentary victory. Still, the savage rage he had felt earlier hadn't left him. It wasn't enough to escape the creature. Chances were that this beast, or another like it, had killed his people.

No, running away wouldn't do at all. He wanted to kill the thing. For that, he needed some sort of weapon, some sort of advantage.

He looked ruefully at his armbands. They had likely saved his life many times over tonight from claws and branches, but they had no offensive capability. But then, he thought, his father had likely planned it exactly that way. Thinking of his father cooled off the battle rage a little and he felt sheepish for craving death. Still, he knew his father would never have imagined him being up against something like this.

There was no use in wishing things to be different. He'd have to work with what he had or what he could create for himself. He headed for some craggy hills in the distance. Maybe he could find a cave or canyon that could be used to set up a trap or ambush.

He thought to press on through the night and spend the day scoping out places for an ambush. But as the sounds of the beast faded to distant silence behind him and his feet grew heavy due to blood loss, he realized he was out of time.

He stopped by the first trickle of a stream he came to and leaned down gingerly to suck at the clear water. Once he had drunk his fill, he lowered his side gently into the water and used his right hand to carefully clean out the wound, gritting his teeth against the pain.

The wound wasn't deep. He hadn't been in danger of breaking ribs or puncturing a lung. That was the good news. The bad news was that the branch had caught and ripped his skin in a large swath. It was a bit like someone had peeled back a large triangle of skin from his side.

The skin would likely re-attach if he could somehow get it to stay in place, but he didn't know how to do that. Every scrap of cloth he could have used for a bandage had been ripped up and tossed about the forest to distract a monster.

As the water settled in his stomach and the adrenaline abandoned him, he realized how tired he was. He dragged himself a small distance from the stream, finding a hollow at the base of a large tree he could crawl into. He held the triangle of skin over the wound and held it closed with his hand, thankful it had stopped bleeding.

As his eyes closed and sleep took him, his fogged mind wondered idly what his child would look like.

# Chapter 6

The morning brought all the wonders of a forest dawn. Birds chirped merrily and the woods seemed to be alive all around him.

This soon proved itself to be all too true as Sadavir found himself the center of attention for a host of bugs that had come to investigate the blood on the leaves. Already, a swarm of larger bugs had gathered around his hand, attempting to investigate the wound underneath.

He brushed them away with a gentle hand. The wound had closed ever so slightly, the chunk of skin holding on its own. He knew how easily it would reopen. Even a fair stretch would have him bleeding again.

Noticing the sun already in the sky, he knew that he had slept much longer than he had intended. His body had taken control, shutting him down while it tried to recuperate from his injury and the terror of the previous night.

Despite how long he had slept, he felt exhausted. The blood loss must have been even worse than he had thought. He was also horribly hungry and thirsty. He eyed the beetles that had gathered around his wound.

Vova had been teaching him some basic survival craft. For all of his fighting skill, Sadavir had still grown up in a warm house with regular home-cooked meals. When he had been banished, the realization of such an obvious blind spot had been a rude awakening. An enemy only had to starve him out to defeat him.

So after everything had calmed down, he had enlisted Vova's help to teach him enough to survive on his own, at least for a little while. Shelters and fire building had come easily enough, and he showed a fair talent for building traps. But Vova taught him that many things weren't possible when you were on the move, and food might be whatever you could stick in your mouth that wasn't poisonous.

Vova had looked on and laughed as he made Sadavir sample various bugs, moss, and bark from a disturbing number of sources. These wouldn't make him feel full or comfortable, Vova had assured him, but they would keep him alive and keep him moving until better could be found.

Still, Sadavir turned away from the bugs that had been poking around his wound. Vova had told him that insects were a wonderful source of fuel for the body, but also a good source of disease or even poison if you picked the wrong ones.

These beetles didn't have the bright coloration

that would suggest poison, but they were entirely too interested in his blood, which suggested they were scavengers, eating dead and rotting things. Such might be disease carriers.

As hungry as he was, Sadavir would welcome a whole plate of bugs, but better to find some that were only interested in eating plants.

His wish was granted entirely too soon. As he crawled out of the hollow, he came face to face with a fat grub, busily munching on a fallen leaf. Sadavir groaned a little on the inside. As much as he wished for the homemade trail biscuits back in his pack, it was a considerable distance in the wrong direction, back at the previous night's campsite.

He didn't know how likely it was that the monster was still in the same area, but he knew he couldn't take any risks, even small ones. With his whole body feeling wracked and weakened, he wouldn't be able to hold out even a single minute against the beast. No, his best bet was to put as much distance between him and his previous campsite as possible.

Having come to his decision, he reached out and plucked up the writhing grub between two fingers. He took only a moment to reflect on the good old days when only people wanted to kill him, then he popped the thing into his mouth, chewed twice, and hurriedly swallowed.

Bits of it seemed to cling to his mouth. He

fought the urge to retch and instead swallowed a couple more times, trying to clear the mess off of his taste buds. He shook his head and hunched his shoulders in a slight shiver of disgust.

One down, dozens to go, he thought to himself, wondering wryly if maybe the risk of death wasn't preferable to this slimy diet. Luckily for him, the rest of his body disagreed with his tongue's assessment. His stomach recognized the mass as food and growled loudly for more. Sadavir dutifully crawled out a little farther and started brushing leaves aside. He found two more grubs, even fatter than the first and they met the same fate.

By now, his gag reflex was threatening dry heaves. He needed water to clear his mouth and throat. Something in the grubs tended to linger and the texture was repulsive. He stood gently, careful to stay hunched over his wounded side. It had healed some, yes, but it had also stiffened during the night. Running was absolutely out of the question.

He hobbled slowly back to the stream he had encountered the previous night and carefully lowered himself down far enough to scoop water up to his mouth. He stayed there for a while, only able to drink small sips at a time from one cupped hand. He held his side with his other hand and didn't want to lay all the way down to put his face in the water. Getting back up would be brutal.

So he stayed there in a crouch, drinking little

swallows of clear water and considering his options. His bloodlust from the previous night had faded, but not completely. There was still some primal part of him that recognized the thing from last night as a threat and rival to be torn apart.

But in the crisp air of morning, his mind was working a little more clearly. His plan last night had been to make it into the rugged hills to the west of him. All he had to do then was to lure the creature into the canyon and drop a boulder onto it. It would be easy enough, the thing hadn't shown incredible intelligence.

He realized now that while his primal side called for blood, he had other matters to consider. He had not come to this land to hunt nightmares. He had come to rescue people. He could see now what had likely happened to them. He steeled his mind to the thought that many, or even all of them, might be dead already.

If there were survivors, he owed it to them to try and find them and bring them home. If they had managed to get away from the beast, their first thought wouldn't have been hunting and destroying the thing, they would be trying to get back to the scaffolding, to get back home.

Sadavir worked through the problem in his mind. He had been following the trail of one of the parties before he had been attacked. It hadn't been much, but he had managed to find a couple campfires that had given him a general direction they had gone. He hadn't seen any signs of struggle or blood, and he certainly hadn't seen any sign of the party coming back on their own trail.

That left the option that they had been cut off from their path home, much like how Sadavir felt cut off from his pack and provisions.

So where would they go? Until he saw their bodies, he had to assume they were alive and moving. They had pairs of crafters on each team, so they would have been able to create shelter or protections very easily. Sadavir knew that Vova's team at least had a pair of light blue Stones. They would be able to seal off a stone wall sufficient to hold off the monster, as long as they had time to do it.

Sadavir had no real evidence that the team he had been following was Vova's. The campfires showed his kind of careful construction, but Sadavir knew that was just wishful thinking. It was the same style all the Destroyers had, nothing wasted or left to chance.

Still, he had to start somewhere, so he decided to think through the problem as if it were Vova's team and there were stone crafters among them. Vova would have likely volunteered himself to lead the monster on a wide looping chase to give the stone crafters a chance to construct something thick and heavy enough to hold back the full force of a creature capable of pushing over trees.

It would take a while, Sadavir realized, for just one pair of crafters to move that much rock. It would take too long. There would be a chance that it wouldn't be done or wouldn't be strong enough to hold by the time Vova came back.

He realized that his friend wouldn't have taken that chance, pinning them all in one location without a quick means of escape. So what solved that problem?

Sadavir groaned in frustration and it came out a growl. His head ached from the blood loss and exhaustion. Thinking only made it worse. It was a problem that was becoming disturbingly familiar. People came to him all the time now with problems and questions. They looked to him as a leader and he had to admit that there was a part of him that enjoyed finally feeling respected after his childhood full of suspicion and dismissal. But he knew deep down that he wasn't as clever as his parents. He certainly couldn't compare to Andre, who seemed to know the answer to everything before anyone even asked.

It had been five years now and Sadavir began to feel like he was hiding a secret. He was a fighter, pretending to be a king. How long before people figured it out and things went back to how they were before?

Sadavir was done drinking now and he started

walking through the woods. He moved slowly, favoring his side. His shuffling gait served the double purpose of stirring up the leaves. Occasionally he would find another of the grubs and choke it down.

The taste and texture didn't get any more bearable, but his stomach welcomed the slimy lumps without so much as a grumble. So Sadavir continued chewing and swallowing with a grim determination. He needed his strength, and he had no way of knowing just how soon he would need it.

Another reason he was walking so slowly was that he still didn't have a destination. He was heading vaguely in the same direction the original path had been pointing, but he was already well off of the trail, so he didn't expect to find any clues.

Around his fifth grub, he got to feeling a little grouchy. It was the beast's fault he wasn't enjoying his mother's flaky biscuits right now, a little voice seemed to growl in his head. It was such a small inconvenience when compared to all the other trauma he had endured; but for some reason, his mushy, wriggling breakfast held a special flavor of injustice.

The more he walked, chewed, and tried to swallow the taste away, the angrier he got at the creature. His bloodlust from the previous night started to re-awaken. By his seventh grub, it took real effort to keep focused on rescuing his friends.

He wanted to trap the thing, to see it die,

crushed below him. He didn't want to be trudging through this forest to nowhere, he wanted to be in the hills. Those rough, craggy hills held promise for him, a chance to gain an advantage. There he could use the terrain to his favor. There would be canyons and drop-offs for ambush, there would be ravines and...

...caves.

There would be caves in those hills, Sadavir realized all at once. With a mountain already covering nearly every side, the stone crafters would only have had to move enough rock to seal the door. That was quite doable, even in a short time frame, assuming they had found a cave with a narrow opening.

Sadavir had already removed the hills from his calculations because he only saw them as a means of attack. But the people fleeing would have seen them in a different light. They could have seen refuge.

He shifted his feet to the new heading and lengthened his stride a little more. He had a destination now, and possibly a chance to rescue his friends and destroy the monster. The morning was definitely looking up. He scooped up one more grub and popped it into his mouth with a grim smile.

Once you got past the little hairs, they weren't really that bad, Sadavir mused.

# Chapter 7

"I don't like it," Aric muttered for the hundredth time. He was at Andre's house. He and Nadya had moved into Aric's village about a month after the unification of the peoples. The two men shared a bond and were often found together, planning out some new invention or arguing over why their latest creation didn't work.

This time, Andre was doing his best to be a good host by himself. Nadya had cleared out shortly after Aric had shown up. Andre couldn't blame her. Lauria had told Aric, in no uncertain terms, to go for a walk after he had complained about the situation a few hundred times in her presence. Andre was getting close to telling him the same thing, but he held back out of sympathy for his friend.

Naturally, Andre didn't like it any better. But the rest of them had been keeping busy, trying to keep their minds off of what might be happening in that strange land that swallowed up their people. Only Aric had gone the other way, fixating on it entirely. His legendary persistence was chewing over the problem like a dog chews on a bone.

Aric paced again, having only occupied his seat

for about thirty seconds since his last pacing trip had concluded. Andre rubbed his temples with both hands. Maybe sympathy was the wrong path, he reasoned to himself. Maybe he would get further by showing Aric that there really wasn't anything he could do.

Like a trapped man seeing a light, he jumped at the possibility.

"So, Aric, what don't you like about it?" Andre asked out loud, giving his friend an easy opening to launch into a real rant instead of his circular muttering.

"Everything!" Aric rose to the bait without hesitation. "I hate everything about it! Are we really so helpless? We control the elements themselves, we have the combined power of two nations! Do we really need to send one man to try and rescue two whole parties?"

Andre knew the question was rhetorical, but he answered it anyway.

"I suppose we could have sent word to some of the other villages. We could have gathered together another rescue party. Maybe that would have been the right decision."

"No, no..." Aric argued, as Andre knew he would. They had to get past the obvious stuff first. "That would have taken too long, maybe even a week or more. Besides, those first two parties had all the courage and expertise anyone could ask for. What could we have sent up that would have made them any better qualified to survive up there?"

"Surely we could have thought of something," Andre offered, another sacrificial sentence.

"Of course we could have. But how long would that have taken? I know Sadavir well enough that he wouldn't have stuck around playing it safe when there were lives at stake. As soon as it was decided that there was real danger, he would feel like he had to leave immediately."

"So we should have gone with him. Or we should go there now." Andre felt good about his conversational strategy. He hadn't had to convince Aric of anything. The big blacksmith was doing it himself, seeing the flaws in all the suggestions.

Really, Andre had no intention at all of leaving his house and climbing that abomination of a structure. Like any reasonable man, he maintained a healthy and understandable fear of being so far off the ground. If a man fell from such heights, he would have time to realize he was dead before it happened. He shivered slightly at the thought.

"We couldn't have gone with him," Aric admitted grudgingly. "He'd need all the edge he could get. I saw him during those battles back in the day. If he had to worry about other people getting hurt, he became far too distracted. It was always a weak spot for him. But if he's got only himself, it's hard to imagine anything that could get past his defenses."

Aric sounded a little smug at this last part. Andre couldn't blame him for that. Aric had really outdone himself with all of the schemes and inventions he had come up with during his son's training.

"So of course we couldn't have gone with him," Aric continued, repeating himself as his eyes started to stare off into the distance. Andre started to tense up. Something was going drastically wrong. He knew that look all too well. It meant that his friend was getting an idea.

Normally, Andre was all for Aric's ideas, but that certainly hadn't been the point of the conversation. There were supposed to be no ideas to be had. Still, Aric's eyes were lighting up with some scheme.

"But what's to say we shouldn't go up there now?" Aric mused. The panic in Andre's eyes grew. His conversational strategy had backfired horribly. He abandoned finesse and went straight to direct opposition.

"Because it's crazy, that's why!" Andre nearly yelled. "What could we possibly do that Sadavir couldn't? We couldn't even expect to do what the first two teams did, and all they really did was get lost!"

"I'm not saying we should go looking for the teams like Sadavir is doing," Aric was talking fast now, as he always did when he got excited about an idea. It didn't matter much if Andre was listening at all. "There's nothing more we can do there, that's true enough.

"But there must be lots of other stuff we could do right there at the top. We could be there to welcome the teams if they find their way back on their own. We could signal Sadavir if that does happen, or we could try to support him in some other way."

"But I..." Andre stammered, but he hadn't actually been able to formulate a real argument, so he sat there with his mouth hanging open, hoping wildly that he would think of one any second. Nothing came. The fact was, it was a great idea to have a supporting team up there. It didn't have to be out in the woods, but it could provide support if support were needed.

Of course, that didn't mean that he wanted to be the one to go. Still, as his brain had been unable to come up with any sort of reason why a support crew shouldn't go up the scaffold, it also failed to provide him with any plausible reason why he shouldn't go along with his friend.

Aric put the decision on him with his next sentence, characteristic of his boundless enthusiasm.

"I'm going. It's the least I can do. It might not even be anything but looking at trees for a while, but if there's even a small chance I could be of some help, I've got to go. Are you with me?"

44

Andre's mouth still hadn't closed. He urged his brain to action, to come up with some valid reason why he should be left out of it. Inwardly, he writhed like a wild animal caught in a trap.

Outwardly, he nodded.

# Chapter 8

Sadavir crossed the trail near nightfall. He had actually given up looking for one and had been trying desperately to find some place to sleep for the night. He had heard a distant crash in the forest about an hour before and he could almost feel the beast's hatred radiating out from the forest. It wasn't near, but it wasn't far, either.

He knew it was only a matter of time before the creature crossed his back trail, picked up his scent, and followed it to wherever he was hiding. He had given himself a little room with which to work.

Earlier in the day, he had failed to see a tree root under some dried leaves and he had tripped. It was a clear sign of exhaustion that he had tripped at all, even more so that he hadn't been able to catch himself. Sadavir, the pinnacle of agility, had toppled and crashed like a toddler struggling with his first steps.

The impact had pulled at his wound and it had started bleeding again. He had laid there a moment, gathering the mental strength to rise back to his feet. When he finally sat up, he saw the mess of bloody leaves he had left underneath him. They gave him an idea and he had gathered all of them up, stirring in a few extra leaves to make a nice collection of bloodstained foliage.

He then walked long false trails, using the leaves to make paths leading off into the woods before backtracking to his original location. He had spent nearly all of the afternoon doing that, building networks of trails, branches off of branches, all of them leading nowhere.

Sadavir held no illusions that he could outrun or outdistance the beast, or that he would be so lucky as to escape its attention. All that remained was to outsmart it.

So as the sun slowly crept towards the hills, he knew that he hadn't crossed much territory. With all of his backtracking and trail making, he had likely only covered the amount of distance he would have covered in an hour or two walking normally, and he had been at it all day.

Going on into the night was completely out of the question. His body felt heavy, each foot like one of his father's anvils. He needed to find a place to lie down before he fell down.

That's when he had found the camp. It hadn't been a camp in the classic sense. There was no campfire or logs pulled around in a circle for people to sit on. What there was were signs of crafting with Stones. A tunnel had been carved into the ground.

Sadavir had chanced upon it while looking for another hollow under a tree.

The tunnel led back under the ground until it opened up into a small burrow, completely surrounded by roots. One more small tunnel led out the other way. Sadavir recognized the reasoning behind the tactic immediately.

The creature could follow the scent to the tunnel opening, but it wouldn't be able to follow inside. It might claw and dig away at the passage, but that would only serve to warn the people within. They were also protected from the creature accidentally crushing them by placing the main cave underneath a tree.

Unless the beast went pushing down all the trees in the forest, there was really no chance of it doing much damage to the sleeping area. Sadavir also noticed that the sleeping area was only big enough for one person.

There had to be more than one alive, or the Stone crafting wouldn't have been possible. That suggested to Sadavir's groggy mind that they must have spread out, minimizing the risk of all of them being taken at once.

These thoughts warmed his mind as he cuddled himself into the man-made cave underneath the tree. At least some of his friends were alive. They were moving, and they were thinking. There was hope.

He blinked at some dirt falling into his eyes and

the next thing he knew he was waking up after sleeping through the night. Underground, he couldn't tell what time it was, but his body cried out with hunger and thirst. He must have been out a long time.

There was a distant part of his brain that felt an odd fascination in what he was going through. He had never pushed himself this hard and for this long. For all his rigorous training and even the battles he had been through, he had never had to go this long, with so little food and water, and after so much blood loss.

In all warriors, there is a morbid curiosity of just what it would take to break them. Sadavir felt it now, not as a conscious thought, but as an itch at the back of his mind. What would his body do if he kept driving it like this? Would he become sick? Would he pass out? Maybe he would lose all reason.

Olya had told him stories of some of the people she had helped in her time as a healer among the Destroyers. Some people were hurt so badly that they went mad for a while, calling out to people who weren't there or thrashing against some enemy only they could feel.

Sadavir hadn't really understood at the time and had nodded along to the stories with no real grasp of what those people were going through. Now as he blinked over and over again to get his eyes to focus, he understood a little better how bad things might get if he came down with a fever or he was wounded again.

But while he understood that such a time might come, it hadn't come for him yet. It took some blinking, but his eyes cleared and focused. It took some gritting of the teeth and slow shuffling, but he worked his way back up to the light of day. He had strength yet.

His step was a little longer on the second day, but more with a sense of panic than a greater sense of strength. His side felt warm to the touch and was getting a little red around the edges. His body was fighting off infection. He knew at least that much of the healing arts. He couldn't see any swelling or pus, and it didn't smell bad, so that was a good sign.

He knew well the danger he was in. He hadn't been able to clean the wound very well or often, and he'd been spending much of his time in the dirt. An infection might take longer to kill him than a hulking demon creature, but he'd be the same dead in the end.

If his wound got infected, there would be little he could do to reverse it. All he could hope to do was to make it back down to the valley floor and get to Olya. That would mean abandoning whoever was left alive up here to the awful things that occupied this land.

So Sadavir grit his teeth a little more against the pain and made short, quick steps, trying to cover more distance. The trail was a little easier to follow now that Sadavir had found the camp. He now saw signs of their passing occasionally, broken branches here, a crumble of gravel there.

He wasn't nearly the tracker Vova was, or any of the Destroyers, really. But it didn't seem like the party was trying to hide their tracks. If anything, they seemed to be purposefully destructive in their path. Likely they knew somebody would be coming to find them eventually.

The thought made Sadavir pause. What would happen if he didn't come back? He could only imagine the mountains his father, mother, and Olya would move to get another rescue party put together. Already he began to picture the faces of the people as the call was made for volunteers. They wouldn't come, obviously.

That left his family pitted against the fear of the people. It was an unstoppable force meeting an immovable object. Sadavir knew his family well enough to know that the unstoppable force would win out. Somehow, his father, or maybe Andre, would talk the people into coming after him.

But how?

Aric was no fool, he couldn't just bully the people into something like that. He'd have to offer them some advantage that made them believe they stood a chance where Sadavir himself had failed.

He would invent something.

# Chapter 9

At that moment, Sadavir was certain, as certain as death itself, that his father was already on his way. Aric wouldn't have waited weeks for his son to return, he would already be worried and coming up with some foolish scheme to rescue the rescuer.

Sadavir started moving quicker. This situation was going to get out of control. There was no way to let the people below know what was going on up here. And none of them had anything in their experience that would allow them to imagine anything like this creature.

He realized that even that type of thinking was optimistic. If there was one creature, there were likely more. For all he knew, there could be vast herds that lived up here, destroying all in their path. His imagination quickly produced dozens of the beasts closing in on him and he found himself nearly jogging as he tried to move more and more quickly.

His task seemed entirely impossible. He had to track down the party he was currently following and affect a rescue. That might involve battling the beast, or many of them. Then he had to get the whole party back to the scaffolding before his father and any fools he might persuade to come with him showed up like lambs to the slaughter.

What were his armbands and acrobatics against such a task? He wished he had Andre's skill with strategy. He wished he had his father's ingenuity. He wished Olya were here.

That last wish brought him up short. Was he really falling that deeply into self-pity that he would wish his pregnant wife to be in this situation? He shook himself, only mentally, as physically shaking would have hurt tremendously. He had to keep his mind on the task at hand.

Getting everything done was impossible, so he was only wasting time and energy worrying about it. He would find the people in the party. That was his next step. Only after he had accomplished that would he worry about how to achieve the next miracle on his agenda.

After walking through the day, he finally came out of the forest and looked out on the ragged hills.

"Finally, a bit of progress," he muttered to himself. Almost as if he had summoned the thing by his optimism, Sadavir heard the distant sounds of crashing and bellowing far behind him.

It wasn't close enough that he should start running, but the sounds suggested that the beast was moving fast. It had likely picked up on his trail. Sadavir felt like kicking himself. He had walked the entire day without leaving any more false trails. He had grown complacent, he realized. He'd gotten lazy and now had put himself into a bad situation.

He looked around him, but there was little he could use to confuse his scent trail. He was out of extra clothing, having already discarded his shirt and having ripped his pants into shorts. Besides, there was a chance that he was already too late. He couldn't move very quickly. By the time he had made a false trail of decent length, he might run into the monster while backtracking his own trail.

Better to try and find cover, he decided. The hills were close. He clamped his hand on the wound at his side to hold it together and launched into a lurching, limping jog. Luckily, the ground between the hills and the forest was smooth and largely uninterrupted by rocks or debris.

Flood plain, Sadavir guessed as he loped along. There were a couple small rivers he could see cutting their way through the hills. When the spring runoff came, he could imagine them converging here at the base of the hills and forming into a small shallow lake during the wet season.

The sound of bulk moving through dense brush was starting to get clearer behind him. He couldn't believe that something that big could move so fast. Still, he wasn't overly worried, he was almost to the hills now.

They looked like everything he had hoped for.

There were crags and caves, cliffs and gullies. He had no doubt that if he could just get into that stone labyrinth, he'd be able to evade the creature. Maybe he could even make a decent fight of it once he was in the right terrain.

The idea brought a grim expression to his pain-drawn face. The anger he had felt at the beast had not left him yet. While he was still focused on finding the other team, there was still a part of him that wanted nothing more than to go to war against the enemy that had wounded him.

He aimed toward a canyon ahead and to his left. It was deep and narrow. It might give him the advantage he needed. He could probably find an offshoot that the beast wouldn't be able to make it into. Or if he managed to find a way to the top of the ridge, the thing might not be able to follow him.

The sounds behind him were getting close. The creature would be clearing the trees any moment, he felt absolutely certain of it. The ground seemed to be rumbling all around him.

A tiny voice in the back of his mind shouted warnings. Something was very wrong. His Stone was swirling with blackness. His instincts were screaming danger at him, but he couldn't pinpoint the source. He knew he was overlooking something, but it was so hard to think with so many things happening all at once.

He already had the monster behind him, about

to clear the forest. There was no cover out here. It would see him immediately and it would be a race into the ravine, though  Sadavir couldn't know for certain he'd even be able to find cover there. Piled on top of that was the aching pain from his side and the bone-deep exhaustion that threatened to steal the agility from his limbs right when he needed it most. It made his body heavy and his mind cloudy.

As if I could think of anything with all that noise, he grumbled internally.

The noise.

He stopped right in the middle of the plain, only about a hundred meters away from the mouth of the narrow canyon that was his aim. Then he listened, trying to catch subtleties above the pounding of his own heart.

It was the rumbling.

The creature behind him was making a racket back in the trees. It likely smelled fresh scent and it was moving faster, heedless of any trees or shrubbery in its way. It was the same mode it had been in during that first night, the pouncing rush of a predator.

For all the noise it was making, however, it wasn't close enough to be rumbling the ground. The vibrations were too pronounced, too near. Something else was in play.

Now that he was holding still, he could hear more clearly. There were extra noises now, and getting louder. They were lower sounds, gratings and poundings. Sadavir turned his head back and forth to try to get a fix on their source.

The realization came all at once like a blow to his stomach. The sounds were coming from the canyon. He started stumbling backwards like a drunken man. Everything told him to retreat, but he had nowhere to go.

It seemed to him that both creatures broke from cover at the same time.. Everything seemed to be happening at once and the utter hopelessness of his situation settled into his mind like a frozen claw gripping his heart.

The one coming out of the canyon hadn't seen him yet. Coming out into the open, it shook its head back and forth. Gigantic nostrils dilated to search for the scent of prey. It had likely heard Sadavir, or heard the other creature and had come out of curiosity.

With the beast out in the open, Sadavir saw that it was even bigger than the one he had been running from the last couple days. The thing was a behemoth, the size of a two story house. It was covered with a thin, gray fur that looked strangely soft, like a mouse's. That's where any similarity to a mouse ended, of course. The broad pads of muscle that made up its body suggested not only power, but something akin to a fleshy kind of armor. No wonder these creatures could throw themselves around without getting hurt.

For all the mass and power, however, the creatures had a long, lanky look to them. If anything, their torsos seemed oddly small compared to their long sweeping arms and legs that gave the things a gangly look. At the end of each arm and leg were a set of three freakishly long claws. The monster in front of him was so big that the claws were as long as swords.

It stood upright on its legs like a man, though it hunched forward and its long arms nearly reached the ground.

Sadavir stood frozen, his mind trying and failing to process the situation. He heard the beast behind him running hard across the open space. It would be on him soon enough and would  make short work of him. It had his scent hot in its nose and it was in full charge.

The creature that had emerged from the canyon looked with rapt curiosity at the other beast that was pounding across the plain. Sadavir had the choice of waiting where he was and being eaten by the one who had been hunting him; or he could run forward and engage the larger one. It was a dismal choice.

A wild idea struck him all at once and he grinned manically at the audacity of it. If he was going out, he might as well go out big. If he had to choose between one or the other...

...he would choose both.

# Chapter 10

He hunched down, ready to bolt. He turned his eyes and studied the nightmare creature coming at him across the plains. It had an absolute focus on him, oblivious that there was a much larger specimen beyond Sadavir.

The timing would have to be perfect. Sadavir felt a surreal calm creep through his mind as he coldly calculated distances and speed. It was a lot like gauging the distance of a jump. He pulled his hand away from his aching side and purposefully stretched at the wound a little.

A stab of pain shot through him while a few drops of blood started to trickle down his side. He grit his teeth against the pain and moved a little more. He would need all his strength for what would happen next. That meant no cringing at his wound, no succumbing to his exhaustion. One last burst before the end.

Finally the creature was close enough. With a lunge, Sadavir was running. His arms were pumping, his legs stabbing at the ground in sharp staccato. His muscles screamed at him and the wound in his side was a gash of bleeding fire. He ignored them all and pushed himself harder.

He covered the first fifty meters in good time. He glanced up at the massive beast he was running towards. It had finally noticed him and was now focusing on him with that same intense hunter obsession. It didn't move, possibly confused by prey that charged right at it.

Sadavir stumbled once and barely caught himself. His clumsiness and the way his breath burned in his throat after only fifty meters were stark evidence of his complete exhaustion. Still he roared in pain and anger to further draw the attention of the one in front of him. The sound wasn't nearly what he had intended. It was closer to a prolonged, hoarse croak than a throaty battle cry.

The creature behind him needed no encouragement. It was already close behind. Sadavir didn't dare look back, but his imagination filled in fangs and claws mere inches from his neck.

The bigger beast took a lunging step forward as Sadavir closed the remaining distance. He was panting with his jaw hanging slack and his tongue hanging out. It was good that the beast had started moving. His run hadn't been as fast as he had planned. His sprint now looked more like a series of trips and stumbles, each one barely caught before he would fall completely. His arms flailed freely, trying to maintain balance for a few more steps.

Luckily for Sadavir's failing body, his final effort had come to an end. The creature's leap brought it within striking distance of Sadavir and it lashed out with both arms, sweeping low with those slicing claws.

It was just as well from Sadavir's point of view. He hadn't been able to run fast enough, the creature behind him nearly stepping on his heels. It was over either way.

He let his feet fail him as the claws came sweeping in. He fell forward through the air, lifting his feet off the ground, barely missing the claws that scraped along the earth to catch at his legs. At the same time, his head and chest fell, dropping beneath the other set of claws that flew grasping above him.

Just like the old mountain of metal bars from his childhood, Sadavir had jumped through the eye of the needle. His body reacted without his command and slipped into a tight roll as he hit the ground. There was no true grace to it, his muscles just didn't know how to do anything else.

If he had had the energy, he could have come out of the roll into another sprint. As it was, he finished the roll on his back, done at last. He felt the blood leaking freely from his side and hoped the end would at least come quickly.

He had done all he could do.

Looking straight up between the two creatures, Sadavir had a unique vantage point for one of the most awe-inspiring things he would ever witness.

The two creatures had both been so focused on him that neither one had let up at all. The two beasts had slammed into each other in a full lunge.

Sadavir had ended up lying slightly below the larger one. If the creatures had been of equal mass, he would likely have been crushed in the melee. As it was, the smaller one hit into the other like a bird smacking into a wall. It fell backwards and writhed in the dirt. It appeared that they had hit head-to-head and the effect was devastating.

While the smaller one couldn't even gain its feet, the larger one had also taken a serious hit and was standing up straight, swaying back and forth, looking unbalanced.

This would have been the moment for an escape, Sadavir realized. His gambit had worked far better than he could have imagined. Unfortunately, he knew that running would be out of the question. He couldn't even stand.

He rolled to his side just a little and looked towards the canyon, more out of curiosity than a real belief in escape. At the edge of the canyon, he saw more gray fur and claws. There were  more of them! He hadn't been running toward refuge, he'd been running into a lair.

Why they weren't joining in the fray, Sadavir couldn't imagine, but it hardly mattered. It was enough to know that every avenue of escape was gone. He rolled back and watched the two creatures as they slowly recovered from their collision. It was only a matter of time before one of them recovered enough to finish him off.

Maybe he'd be fortunate and pass out before that happened. The blood was flowing again from his side and he was making no effort to stop it this time. He felt lightheaded and a faint blue light twinkled at the corner of his eye, like a piece of the sky had chipped off and had fallen among the crags.

The larger beast recovered first. It looked down at the other creature that had run into it and bellowed. The sound vibrated Sadavir's bones. He had heard something similar on the first night he was attacked, but this reached new levels. He couldn't imagine such a low tone carrying such immense volume. It was as if the force of the noise itself would be enough to shake Sadavir to pieces.

The roar had an invigorating effect on the smaller beast. It finally got its feet under it, but it didn't stand up like the other one. It stayed on all fours, the long arms and legs giving it a spidery look. It roared back its defiance bravely enough, and attempted a quick grab at Sadavir.

This enraged the larger one and it swatted the hand away roughly, stepping forward aggressively. This brought it face to face with the smaller one. It also brought one of its back feet right up by Sadavir, the massive claws gripping at the dirt with the sharp tension that comes before a fight.

All the exhaustion had brought Sadavir's mind to a dreamlike state. He saw the intense, violent happenings above him like mist images. In this detached state of mind, he wondered why the claws weren't digging deeper into the soil. It certainly felt soft enough beneath him, but the massive claws were only sinking a few inches into the ground.

Must be rocks, he mused softly to himself, grinning at his cleverness for solving the mystery so quickly. The pain in his side had faded. He was only vaguely aware of swift motions above him. The smaller beast hadn't backed down, and now the larger one was puffing itself up, roaring again while slashing at the smaller one, though the bellowing didn't sound loud to Sadavir's fading senses.

He turned his mind back to the question of the rocks. His dreamy thoughts found the subject far more interesting than the battle above. It would make sense if the flood plain had had most of its soil washed away over the years. If there was a quick exit for the water, the sediment would be washed away to gather at a lower point. He might be laying only a few inches away from bedrock. He wished he had enough energy to dig down and see for himself.

He turned his head back the other way to look at the creature's back foot. If it were as shallow there, maybe that would be proof that this was mostly a sediment shelf. Sure enough, the back foot also only penetrated a few inches. And there was that blue light again.

It wasn't at the corner of his vision now, it was right in the center. It looked like it was coming right out of one of the hills. Some distant part of his brain whispered to him that it was important, but his thoughts were like fish in a pond, wandering aimlessly.

Something wet and warm splashed over him. He craned his head casually to look at his chest. It was covered in blood. This seemed perfectly all right to him. This was the right setting for blood. It felt like a battle, swift motions, violent actions, the smell of dust and blood. He wondered if he would be stepped on. It certainly seemed plausible.

That's when the earth opened up and swallowed him.

# Chapter 11

His next memories were foggy. Images jumbled together in random order, as if his memories had all been written on leaves that had blown all over his mind. There was stone and earth, moving around him like giant cradling arms. Rumbling like thunder, but with no rain or lightning.

Time passed like a dream, years and minutes blending naturally. He saw visions of Olya, felt her strong arms holding him and he smiled. Then he dreamed of Vova, angry with him and jostling him around like a bully. Other faces came and went, some had sharp edges and drawn faces. Others were fuzzy and ethereal and smiled at him with perfect carelessness.

This alloy of reality and dreams carried him through time he couldn't feel or measure. Still, even without context or scope, time passed and things changed. The boundaries between reality and hallucination started to assert themselves once more. Sadavir was sad to see Olya go, but another part of his brain rejoiced knowing that she was safe.

As the dreams faded, the pain came back. There

was a dull aching in his side that became more and more insistent, demanding his attention, though there was nothing he could do for it. Finally came the brightness of consciousness, though it wasn't quite as bright as Sadavir had remembered it.

There was no sun, only flickering light dancing on stone walls. His glazed eyes studied the wall curiously as his brain slowly awakened and put everything in its place. The wall wasn't the source of the light, a fire was. A fire that must be behind him, as he couldn't see it. He became aware that he was lying on his right side.

He turned slowly to the left, being very careful not to pull at the pain that seemed to be sleeping there. He went as far as his back, then turned his head to look at the fire. It was small, but hot, built in the Destroyer fashion. Behind the fire was a row of anxious faces, watching him.

His eyes focused slowly, the faces turning from blurry shapes to a random assortment of eyes, noses, and mouths; and finally to recognizable features that brought memories crashing back. Vova was there, right at the center of the small crowd.

"Vova," he said, or tried to. The breathy growl that actually came out bore little resemblance to his friend's name. His throat was drier than he had ever felt it. Suddenly, breathing seemed hard, like his parched throat was about to collapse into dust.

Luckily, he didn't have to voice his need.

Anxious hands were already lifting his head and cool, brackish water was being poured in a tiny trickle down his throat. At first, his muscles wouldn't respond as they should and he had to let the water sit at the back of his throat, slowly trickling down on its own. Finally, he coughed and he swallowed out of reflex.

His body remembered its normal functions and he started actively sipping at the water, grateful for the new feelings of life it carried with it. His body seemed to absorb the water like a sponge, his dried out fibers swelling back to their normal sizes.

When he tried to move, however, he found that the feelings of rejuvenation were premature. His whole body ached and his muscles responded only with extreme protest.

"Take it slow," one of the voices needlessly advised him. "You've lost an incredible amount of blood. By rights you should be dead."

Pink light glowed around him and he felt the pain lessen. The pink Stones had healing abilities. It was nothing near to what Olya could do. When Olya healed someone, it was an act of creation. Torn fibers became whole, toxins and fevers vanished, and the whole system was brought back to what it should be under the glow of a perfect light.

The pink Stones worked with the body itself, prompting it to lessen swelling, ease pain, and quicken healing. There were always natural limits to
68

how quickly the body could repair itself. Still, Sadavir knew he would be dead without their efforts and he felt a deep gratitude for their ministrations.

Still, he felt all the urgency of his last remembered moments. Everything was so confused in his mind that he was having a hard time separating delusion from reality.

"Vova."

His voice was scratchy and he could only manage a whisper, but it was good enough. Vova moved closer and patted Sadavir on the shoulder.

"I'm here," Vova reassured Sadavir. "Though I can't believe you're here too! I'm sorry it took us so long to rescue you, but we could hardly believe what we were seeing. How in the world did you ever get into such a position?"

"Long story," Sadavir mumbled, though he realized it was a short story he didn't feel like telling yet. "How long have I been out?"

"Around three days."

"Three days?" Sadavir jerked as if to stand up, but his body assured him it was still too early for that. "How could I possibly have been out for three days?"

"The healers are saying that your wound was starting to get infected. Combine that with the impressive blood loss and you're lucky you didn't slip completely into a coma or worse."

Sadavir suddenly felt very weak indeed. A

shudder went through him as he realized how close he had been to dying. Even with all the combat he had seen, he had never felt death as close as he did now, even though the actual moment of danger has passed. What truly galled him was how easily it had happened.

While the creatures were fierce, he would have died without being killed by them directly. He had simply received a wound of moderate severity and had been pressed hard enough that he was never able to tend to it. Suddenly he felt very mortal.

"I'm here to rescue you," Sadavir said, immediately aware of how ludicrous the statement was. Vova smiled broadly and squeezed his shoulder.

"Do that hear that, everyone?" he said a little louder. "We are saved!"

A couple light chuckles echoed around the small cave. But it was a subdued noise, a token bit of humor. The truth was that too many people were missing. The original party had been close to twenty people, Sadavir saw less than ten scattered around the cave. Even Vova's determined humor wasn't enough to lift their spirits to more than a courtesy laugh.

If he hadn't been lying on his back, Sadavir would have hung his head. It was a sorry sight. These were some of the best and brightest both peoples had to offer. Now they looked like beaten refugees, huddled in a cave lit only by the flickering light of a few oil lanterns.

"I'm so sorry for the people you've lost. More sorry that I've only added to your burden. Not much of a rescue, I fear, but I had no idea what I was going to be up against."

"It could have been a lot worse," Vova returned. "We managed to find sign of the torqs before they found us. We at least knew to expect something big. We still weren't ready for just how big, but we were at least being as careful as we could."

"Torqs?" Sadavir interrupted.

"Those big beast things you were trying to wrestle out there. I forget sometimes that you had a Creator education. We named them after a breed of demon found in our myths. They were punishing devils with swords welded onto both hands. It seemed fitting for these animals."

Sadavir gave a weak nod.

# Chapter 12

"What happened?" he asked.

"They came on us all at once one morning..."

"They? You had more than one attack you?"

"Yes, two of them came straight at us. One of them was the big alpha you were lying under when we scooped out a hole and dropped you in it. Lucky for us, the rest of the herd held back. They're very hierarchical, these things."

"Herd?" Sadavir mumbled the question, not fully wanting to hear the answer.

"Oh yes," Vova nodded emphatically. "This alpha commands a herd of no less than ten females. He allowed one of them to accompany him on the hunt that morning. We had defenses set up around our camp, traps and tripwires and such.

"Still, it wasn't enough. It barely slowed the things down. If anything, the obstacles enraged them even more. Our only advantage was that it gave us a little bit of a warning."

"Were you able to fight them?" Sadavir asked. Vova shook his head. He held silent for a while, gathering his emotions. The question had struck a nerve, something powerful, and Sadavir gave his friend the time he needed to gather himself.

"With the warning we had, we could have escaped. I was the one who made the call to stand and fight the things. I underestimated the enemy and my friends died for it."

Vova's confession was little more than a whisper. He had always been a passionate man, a person bound by absolute ideals. Sadavir could only imagine what burdens Vova was carrying at that moment.

"You couldn't have known..." Sadavir started to comfort his friend, but Vova cut him off sharply before he could finish.

"That's exactly it!" he spat. "I didn't know enough, but I made the call anyway. I should have played it safe until I knew more. This is new country, new dangers. I knew they were big, but I had assumed that they would be heavy, plodding creatures. That assumption cost lives."

"So what happened after the attack?" Sadavir pushed the conversation forward, as much to save Vova from dwelling on it as to gather more information.

"The first scuffle was brutal," Vova continued his narrative. "We had a couple of those launchers your father had made. We figured it would be more than enough to take down any creature out there. Unfortunately, while they did sting the creatures quite a bit, it didn't take them down.

"We lost the launchers in the first sweep. I had one, and Sasha had the other. We stood our ground until we saw the thing bearing down on us, then we both fired at the same time. I guess it stung enough that the thing stumbled and roared. Then the arm swept out. I couldn't believe that any animal could have such reach. It hit Sasha first, killing him in the first blow.

"It was his body that saved me, because that's what slammed into me instead of the claw. It knocked me sprawling. Luckily, I managed to scurry around a tree and duck into a hollow. The thing had my scent and came hunting me. These things get a scent in their nose and it's like the rest of the world stops.

"If I'd been on my own, it would have killed me right away. As it was, my team was focused on me and was crafting both the tree and the earth around it to give me constant, changing cover. It was more than the beast could adapt to or figure out.

"But while they were focused on saving me from the alpha, they failed to protect themselves. The second monster came out of the woods like death itself. It tore into the group and ripped them apart. I have never seen carnage like that. I always imagined it would look like that if you were to turn your Stone against a crowd of people."

Sadavir shuddered at the image. When he held both Olya's Stone and his own, with Olya there to add her will to the power, it was a pure destructive force, even more drastic and powerful than Olya's healing. Sadavir turned his attention back to Vova as he continued his story.

"I ordered retreat immediately. We tore out through the woods, drawing close together. At first, it seemed like we had lucked out. The creatures didn't follow us. It was only later that we realized it was because they already had their meal."

Sadavir felt chills run down his spine from the bitterness in Vova's voice. He could feel the hatred in it, and he could relate to the anger. More similarities revealed themselves as Vova continued his story.

"We lost more people almost right away. We started running away back towards the scaffolding. That's when we came upon the herd. They all saw us and charged. That would have been the end of us. As it happened, the alpha still had my scent. So while it had paused for a short while to eat, it had already returned to hunting us.

"It found us right as the rest of the herd came charging. When he roared at them, the others backed off. He had claimed us, or at least me. That's the same thing you saw when you brought those two alphas together. They both claimed you and that led to a fight. That was good thinking!"

Sadavir did his best to shrug.

"To be honest, I didn't know they were going to do that. I figured I was dead and wanted it to be as big as possible."

Vova stared at his injured friend with a mix of incredulity and wonder.

"You're a special kind of crazy, you know that? Dead is dead, my friend. You didn't even know anyone was watching. Why would you care about a grand ending if there was no one there to witness it?"

"Do you remember my Uncle Amar?"

"Yes, nice enough guy. I never did understand why he left, or even where he went."

"It's hardly important now. But he always said he followed me around to witness a story. I guess part of that mentality rubbed off on me. I can't help but see my life as he did, as a story. And a story deserves a good ending, even if the story is never told."

Vova didn't answer right away, giving the response the respect it deserved. He finally nodded slowly.

"I can understand that. I might have to borrow that idea from you, it might make some of this a little easier for me."

"Go for it. Anyway, what happened next? How did you escape the alpha?"

Sadavir felt a little sorry for asking, as his friend had cheered up slightly at their philosophical discussion. Now, his expression fell back to the deep depression that had marked his face during the telling of his tale.

"More people died. We ran and we crafted obstacles as we went. It slowed him down enough that we were able to put some distance between us and him. That's when we figured out that they hunt by smell. We had put enough distance between us that we should have been safe. Instead, he came straight to us.

"Rather, I should say he came straight at me. We had slowed down and spread out a bit, looking for water and a decent campsite. We still had wounded at that time, so we desperately wanted to find a place to stop and treat the wounds.

"I was well off to the left, separated from the main group. The alpha came straight at me, even before it could see me. There was another chase through the woods. The others came to help me and one of our wounded, Kolya, attracted its attention long enough for it to kill him and the person helping him. Those were our last casualties.

"We've managed to stay ahead of them, though only barely. I brought what was left of the team to these hills. I figured they could give us some more permanent shelter. I also thought we might be able to figure out some sort of advantage. Maybe we could figure out an ambush and start killing some of these things."

Vova made no attempt to hide the hatred in his tone. Sadavir was a little surprised to hear his own thoughts and feelings spoken out loud by another person so precisely. But then, Vova had lost much more than Sadavir had. He had seen his friends die, ripped apart and even eaten by these monsters. He had even more reason to feel anger towards the things.

"Have you had any luck?" Sadavir asked.

"Very little," Vova shrugged. "While we're safe in our cave, the things have kept right on top of us, so we haven't had much room to move or plan. So most of the time we've spent in here, seeing to the wounded. We've managed to make a few scouting trips and we've learned a bit more about them. We were out on one such trip when they suddenly all headed towards the canyon.

"We started moving everyone, thinking maybe it was our opportunity to escape, or at least make it to a better strategic location. Imagine our surprise at seeing you caught between two of the things and charging one like you were going to attack!

"You know, for half a heartbeat, I almost believed it. That should concern you, Sadavir, if people can actually believe that you're crazy enough to take on one of these things!"

Vova chuckled to show Sadavir it was all in good fun and clapped him on the shoulder. Sadavir only smiled wanly in response. The joke wasn't too far from the truth. In fact, there was a part of him, and not a quiet part, that wondered what such a contest would look like. Maybe if he weren't surprised and had had all his strength about him...

They were dangerous, insane thoughts.

"So what's the plan now?" Sadavir asked, getting his mind back to their present predicament. Vova's hand responded first to the question, pressing down meaningfully on Sadavir's shoulder.

"All plans are on hold until your side is healed. We'll do all we can to get ready, but we'll need you in order to make it back to the scaffolding, and you aren't going to be much good to us with your ribs practically hanging out in the open air. So we're all going to wait until you're healed before we do anything else."

Sadavir endeavored to sit up so he could argue face to face. When he failed in the attempt, he realized his friend might have a point. He settled back down to wait.

# Chapter 13

"Come on, Andre, you're going to have to let go eventually!" Aric urged his friend.

"I don't know what evidence led you to that conclusion," Andre muttered through clenched teeth. "Right now it seems perfectly reasonable to me that I stay right here and die of hunger. I would choose that a hundred times over before I'd choose plummeting to my death from this rickety contraption."

In reality, the scaffolding they were climbing was remarkably sturdy. The solid construction was engineered and reinforced in dozens of creative ways. There could have been an army jumping up and down on it at every level and it wouldn't have created anything more than a vibration in the structure.

But none of these logical thoughts meant anything to Andre at the moment. He had been brave for hours, climbing this death trap of bars and platforms. Then, when he started to relax a little, he had decided he would face his fears and take a glance over the edge.

He had taken special care all this time to keep

his eyes either looking up or at the wall. But as bad luck would have it, right as he looked down, a rogue gust of wind swept by and shifted his balance by the sheer unexpectedness of the moment. While he was never in real danger of going over the edge, it had been enough to feel himself lose control while looking at the hundreds of feet of nothingness beneath him.

He had latched both arms around the nearest pole and held on with more fervor than he had ever shown to his wife or children, and Andre was a loving husband and father. His mind had made the connection that this pole was the only thing keeping his fragile human body from crashing down to the ground. So he held onto it, and Aric's logic was a weak counterbalance to his panic.

Aric, who had also been very nervous at the beginning, had been gaining in both courage and impatience as they neared the top. So he had scolded, bribed, and even threatened Andre trying to get his friend to release his grip on the pole. Nothing had worked and now Aric was pondering more direct methods.

His son was up there, almost certainly in real danger. Surely Andre would understand if Aric had to physically pry his hands off the pole. A finger or two might break, but he was successfully convincing himself that Andre would forgive him eventually and one day they'd even laugh about it. The idea was becoming morbidly appealing the longer the standoff dragged on.

He was about to do a test pull on an exposed thumb when inspiration struck him. His smile was a wicked thing to behold. Andre tensed even more upon seeing it, having already sensed the possibility of his large blacksmith friend turning violent on him.

"What are you up to?" Andre asked, his voice almost a whimper.

"I'm thinking I'll leave you here," Aric's grin widened a little more, a cat smiling at a trapped bird. Andre actually relaxed a little as Aric had already used this ploy. It hadn't worked before and it wasn't going to work now. The fear of being left alone meant nothing compared to his trepidation before the endless space beneath him.

"Yeah, I'd understand that. Hey, you do what you've got to do. Go help your boy, I'll be right here when you come back down" Andre muttered, closing his eyes tightly against a sudden dizzy spell.

"Oh, I'm not going up. I think I'll go back down."

"Down?" Suspicion was back in full force.

"Oh yes. There's not too much I can do without your help up there, so there's no reason to continue upward. I can think of a couple reasons to head back down without you, though."

"Such as?"

"Nadya. I think your wife should hear the story about how you chickened out halfway up and sat down and cried like a little baby for hours and hours."

82

"Hey! I haven't cried at..." Realization hit him like a club to the forehead. The dizziness was suddenly gone and holding onto the pole was becoming a lower priority by the second. His eyes narrowed. "You wouldn't!"

"Oh yes I would," Aric assured him calmly, confident in his trap. "If there's one thing I learned from my friend Amar, it's that stories have a great deal of power. Whether they're true or not is fairly inconsequential."

Andre's grip loosened a little more. Maybe he had been hasty, he reasoned inwardly. After all, he could only die once; but if Nadya ever heard about this, he would hear about it for the rest of his life. He could already see his wife's mocking smile as she politely offered to get things for him from the top shelf, since they were so high and all.

It would be a harsh contrast to his farewell. She had been so proud of him, so brave and selfless. To have the rest of the story end in humiliation was starting to look a lot more horrifying than a mere plunge to oblivion. He turned dark eyes onto Aric.

"This is one story that never gets told, understand? Never!" He let go with one hand to turn and face his friend defiantly, though he kept one arm around the pole, as if he were holding it hostage.

"You come with me and I'll carry it to my grave," Aric promised solemnly. Andre let his other arm slip away from the pole.

"There's something wrong with you, you know that? You won't stop at anything and you never know when you're beat. That's a dangerous combination, old friend."

Aric shrugged, but didn't deny the accusation.

"If I had given up because I was beaten, then Sadavir would have been killed as a baby and your people would still be shut out on the far side of a wall. I might be dangerous, and I might hurt people someday. I've always known that. Still, I can't give up on my son..."

Aric stepped forward and placed a hand on the smaller man's shoulder.

"...and I'm not giving up on you."

Andre smiled in spite of himself. Aric had a way of inspiring loyalty, even while blackmailing him.

"Then let's go get your boy."

# Chapter 14

The next couple weeks were torture for Sadavir, though the pain had little to do with his physical wounds. He was accustomed to pain and hardship. He had grown up on it like mother's milk. But this was the first time in his life he had ever been forced to do nothing.

Other people in the party made scouting trips to keep track of the monsters and to forage any kind of food they could find. They had plenty of food that they had packed along, especially since the number of people it had to feed had been reduced significantly. Still, people get tired of dried meat and dehydrated tubers, so any sort of fresh fruit or vegetables the searchers could bring back was met with enthusiasm.

Many times, the scouts came back in a rush, the huge creatures right on their heels. While they hadn't lost anyone else, these were still frightening times. They were reminders to all of the people in the cave that they were being actively hunted by vicious things that weren't going away and weren't giving up.

Vova did all he could to help mollify Sadavir's restlessness, but there wasn't much that could be done. Every time the creatures got close, Sadavir would tense up, his heart beating faster and his breath quickening. Anyone who didn't know him might mistake these as symptoms of fear.

Vova knew better.

He knew that what got Sadavir's blood pumping was a desire for battle. These things had beaten him, left him broken and bleeding in a way he had never experienced before. The emotions driving him would no longer be concern for the safety of others. Sadavir wanted revenge.

Vova couldn't blame him, of course, though he was worried that Sadavir would run straight at the things and get himself killed. So the two of them spent hours every day talking strategy and tactics. Thousands of options were brought up, discussed, torn apart, and put back together again. Some seemed viable, some less so, most were outright crazy.

The most immediate concern was how to get away from the herd that had them cornered in this cave. Their persistence was the most troubling thing of all. Almost any predator will slink off to find other prey if thwarted in its original attempts at capture. This obsessive behavior added a level of danger that was difficult to plan around.

With the careful ministrations of the healers,

Sadavir was at least healed of the major wounds by the end of the first week, though he was still weak. The next week he spent gathering his strength again, pushing himself hard every day to exercise in the limited space of the cave. He ate double his rations of dried meat every day to build his stamina and energy back to battle-ready. No one ever questioned the extra food or even suggested that he take it easy. There was a light in his eyes that scared people a little, so they held back and offered whatever support he asked of them.

At the end of two weeks, he declared himself ready to go. As always, no one argued, even though the scar on his side was still fresh and raw. The pain and physical trials had given Sadavir something of a gaunt look, ribs showing and dark spaces under his eyes; but it only made him scarier. It was like watching a hungry wolf, made even more dangerous by being backed into a corner.

"We're getting out of here tomorrow," he announced. "It's time to get you people back home."

"So how do you want to do it?" Vova asked, careful to make his question sound like support, rather than a challenge.

"How close are they?" Sadavir asked. One of the scouts, Pasha, offered the information.

"They're all around us. They've figured out that we're in here. We've had to craft a new opening almost every time we leave because they're already waiting and scratching at the stone of every tunnel we've created. We've got the entire herd huddled around us now."

"Perfect," Sadavir stated with dark conviction. "We've baited them long enough, it's time we sprung our trap."

"What trap?" Vova asked. It didn't sound like any of the plans they had talked over recently and he felt a little perturbed that Sadavir had made the decision without him. "We haven't been working on anything. If we were supposed to, then you should have told us earlier than this. These things take time."

"We have our trap all ready to go," Sadavir assured his friend. "We've been sitting in it this whole time."

Vova's eyes widened as comprehension dawned. They had explored similar ideas, but nothing this specific. Sadavir continued to explain for the benefit of everyone else in the room.

"This cave is our trap. They are going crazy out there, I've heard them. They're dying to get in here. All we have to do is give them a way in."

Some people nodded along, grasping the concept. Some of the Creators seemed to be having a hard time with the idea however. Creators were very straightforward thinkers, it was one of the things that helped them be so successful in their various trades. It also made it difficult for them to see strategy,

88

especially strategies that involved letting huge nightmare beasts into the only refuge they had.

"First, we bleed," Sadavir expanded. "Vova, I need your blood especially. We need to make sure the alpha out there is willing to do anything to get in here."

Vova had already seen this coming and walked up to the stone slab where Sadavir had spent so much of the last couple weeks. A quick draw of a sharp blade across the back of his forearm got blood dripping onto the rough stone.

Sadavir let his eyes wander the room, making eye contact with every person as he went. Each one that met his eyes eventually dropped their gaze and stepped forward to join Vova at the slab. More blood joined Vova's and soon everyone except Sadavir had contributed. The cloying, metallic smell of blood hung in the cave and a few of the people looked like they might be sick.

Nobody wanted to look at the slab now, their eyes searched corners of the room or found each other in the dimmer light. With the added blood, the slab looked like a sacrificial altar, fresh with the blood of victims. It was too powerful a reminder of what they had been through and what they were likely to face.

Still, it seemed like the distant scratching coming from outside on the hillside was becoming more insistent. The monsters were taking the bait.

The smell of blood would drive them crazy for the next little while, which was exactly what Sadavir wanted.

"Next, we craft the tunnels larger. These torqs are large, but they're also pretty skinny. I think they could fit in here if the openings were just a little larger. Leave the blocks on the passage openings, but widen everything else, especially where you can hear them scratching. We need every one of them to have a space to squeeze into."

"And where will we be when all of this goes down?" asked Vova.

Sadavir pointed a finger upwards. He almost seemed to be pointing at the oil lantern hanging above his head.

"We're going to be right above them."

# Chapter 15

"That ought to do it!" Andre announced. Really, Aric was the one holding the Stones and crafting excess steel into a tower, so it should have been his call as to whether the structure was done or not. Andre might have been a little anxious to have the project over with. Just looking at the thing made him shudder.

"Oh, don't be so hasty," Aric started, then amended his advice once he turned and saw his friend's blanched face. "And don't be so scared, I used a similar design when I built Sadavir's climbing cage. It held me fine and you're much lighter than me."

Andre knew all of this, of course. They had been over everything and Andre had even added his own touches, reinforcements that would make the tower even more stable. Still, looking at the thing on the windy edge of the cliff did odd things to his stomach.

It was only the latest of a series of improvements they had been working on since they had reached the top. Aric had wanted to build the tower first. He had seen it as a more direct way to look for his son. Andre had convinced him that actually trying to follow Sadavir off through the wilderness was equal parts pointless and insane.

He had then capitalized on that victory of reason to convince Aric that the first thing they should build was some sort of defensive weapon. So they had done so. It stood behind them now. It was a scaled up version of the stone launchers that the party had taken along. It was larger and stood on a stand instead of being held in hand.

It had also been modified to be MUCH louder. Aric had built it in such a way that the mechanism that drove the projectile also slammed two iron sheets together at the end of the propelling drive. The effect was an ear-splitting clang that could likely be heard for miles. He had reasoned that most things they would be defending themselves against would be wild animals, afraid of the noise. Also, if more time passed and they hadn't heard from Sadavir, they could start firing it off periodically as a kind of signal.

They hadn't fired it off at all yet. They were working near the edge of the cliff every day and Andre's nerves were shot. He had told Aric in no uncertain terms that experimental, ground-shaking noise makers were off limits for the near future.

"Still, you're right," Aric agreed. "I think that's about all we can do. Would you like to try it out?"

The question was asked with a teasing smile. Andre only glared back at him in answer.

92

"Ok, ok! I'll try it out first."

Aric turned back to the tower and took a deep breath of his own. While he wouldn't let Andre see it, he was a little scared himself. The thing did look a little rickety. They had been limited on metal. They had brought some up with them and some had been "borrowed" from the scaffolding, but they had used most of what they had in building the weapon.

What was left over wasn't quite enough to build a decent tower. So they had relied heavily on engineering to add strength to the structure, small struts and joists that combined synergistically to make the whole structure sound, even if each piece was weak.

These things made perfect sense in Aric's mind, and he wasn't about to let fear hold him back. Still, standing at the base of it made him more than a little nervous. They had set it near the edge of the cliff because the rock was bare there and made for a much better foundation and anchor for the structure. That, combined with the thin construction, gave the whole thing the appearance of something about to be blown over the edge by any passing breeze.

All of these thoughts passed through Aric's mind in a moment, not long enough to let Andre think he was hesitating. Then his beefy hands were gripping the bars and he was climbing. He grit his teeth against the sound of creaking metal that accompanied every step.

Step over step and hand over hand brought him slowly above the height of the trees and then a little higher. He found a good spot to settle in near the top and took a good look around.

Stretched out in front of him like a giant fan was a sprawling forest. Aric hadn't seen many forests, but something about this one seemed a little wrong to him. He couldn't put his finger on exactly why, but there was a kind of raggedness to it. The patterns suggested that if he could get high enough, he'd see large bare patches like on a sickly animal. Far to the west, the horizon was bumpy and broken. It could be hills or low mountains, but he couldn't see well enough to know for sure.

To the east, the forest thinned and gave way to plains. Aric could see the glimmer of a large lake right at the edge of his vision to the northeast.

Just to the south of that lake was nothing, a large patch of land that was completely devoid of trees or vegetation. It almost seemed to have a gray tint to it. Maybe rocks, he thought, though the gray parts seemed to move a little, so maybe it was a gray kind of grass, waving in the wind as it does on the plains. He blinked a time or two and rubbed his eyes, but it was just too far away for him to pick out any more detail.

The grayness worried him. Maybe it was some kind of blight or poisonous plant that permeated this land. He had been all too confident, sending Sadavir

94

up here. He knew that Sadavir could handle any sort of battle, but what if this wasn't a fight at all? What if the danger up here was plague or poison? The thoughts weighed heavy on Aric's mind as he scrambled back down the tower.

"I think we should stay close to the cliffs," Aric remarked glumly. It was a harsh concession for him to make, especially as he had been intending to try and persuade Andre to at least make a few short scouting runs with him once he had the lay of the land.

Andre nodded silently, recognizing at once his own victory, but also realizing what that had taken from his friend. So he simply agreed and asked no further questions.

# Chapter 16

The new day dawned; though there was no brightness in the dark cave to mark the difference between night and morning. There was only a tense energy in the air, an equal mixture of anxiety and anticipation. It was doubtful that anyone had slept.

Those with light blue Stones had worked all through the night, crafting larger tunnels for the creatures and a small, steep escape tunnel that led upwards through the mountain.

Now the time had come and the party was divided into small teams, each one huddled around a lantern. All eyes were on Sadavir. He knew he should feel anxious. He had certainly felt anxiety all those years ago when he had first been called upon to lead people.

That wasn't the case now. He felt no butterflies in his stomach, there was no lump in his throat, and his heart beat at a steady pace. He felt strong again and with that strength came a desire for redemption. He wanted to erase the shame of his brutal beating, to forget the fear that had driven him to panic.

He nodded to the assembled crowd. It was far

smaller than it should have been, a handful of people who had been cowering in the dark for far too long. He didn't feel up to a big, inspiring speech, and the plan had already been discussed in depth. So he went with something simple:

"Stick together. We're going to get through this."

He waved the party forward into the escape tunnel and they started the climb. He headed down one of the wide tunnels where he could hear the most scratching. The doors were blocked by large slabs of stone that had been crafted to fit snugly into the mountain. Last night, they had been modified to be reinforced primarily by a thin, slanted column of stone. It was this column that Sadavir now shattered with a heavy club.

The heavy block didn't fall out of the way immediately, but it did start to move in response to the urgent scratching on the other side. Dust and pebbles began falling away from the edges as it started to work free. The beast on the other side had heard the crash of the column and now felt the sudden weakness in the barrier. The clawing became more insistent.

Sadavir dashed away, down to the next tunnel. There he repeated the process, with the same effect. He went from tunnel to tunnel, knocking down supports and freeing the blocks. He could already hear the sound of a block being hauled away from the first tunnel. He had to be quick.

As he broke the supporting column on the last tunnel, the block didn't just budge, it blew inward with incredible force. Sadavir rolled backward out of the way and came back onto his feet, blinking away the dust and staring right into the face of the alpha. Powerful claws shot down the corridor after him and Sadavir dodged them, using his left armband to turn one sword-like claw away from his body and into the wall.

It felt right. It felt like the clash of battle and his pulse surged in his ears. He rolled backwards again, dodging another attack. The creature's motion was limited by the narrow corridor and Sadavir was back in full control. Without their full range of motion, these creatures were no match for Sadavir's agility and Stone-enhanced reflexes.

So Sadavir took his time, taunting the creature and leading him deeper into the cave. The corridor started to press on the creature and it was nearly stuck. It might have even turned back, but as it got nearer to the center of the cave, the more it smelled the blood on the stone slab.

Sadavir remembered what Vova had said about these things fixating on a single victim. Likely, this alpha had smelled Vova's blood by now and was now cramming itself wildly into the rocky passage, trying to get at the prey that had escaped it.

Other creatures had broken through now. Some

of them were smaller and were nearly into the center portion. Still, their motions were severely limited and Sadavir danced through their swiping attacks with contemptuous ease.

He rolled and jumped through the room, darting in and out of corridors. One of the smallest creatures had managed to work its way entirely into the center room and kept trying to stand up, though the roof was far too low to allow it. There was a rumbling now as rocks tumbled from parts of the roof and passageways. The creatures were straining furiously at a structure that had already been weakened and perforated by lots of tunnels.

The last beast finally broke its barrier and shot through the passageway. This was the smallest one of all, which is why it had been last to break through. Its small size gave it extra mobility, though, and it was able to shoot through the passage to where Sadavir was now dodging claws and teeth at every step.

It barreled into him in a blind rush. Sadavir had been evading another swipe from the alpha, which had one arm into the room, but had the rest of its body stuck fast in the passage.

The mass hit him and he was sent flying right into the back of another beast. Only the darkness saved him. The creatures were swatting blindly around for him, but they were coming in from the sunlight. Sadavir had been in the relative dark for two weeks and his eyes were well adjusted to the half-light. Naturally, it helped that his Stone required no light at all to fuel his reactions. Many times, Sadavir moved only on instinct, not knowing why he was jerking or swinging his armband in the dark.

These instinctual movements had saved his life every time. He had learned from his training to trust his Stone. If there was something to be destroyed, his Stone would lead him to the how of it.

Of course, as he had discovered during his first interaction with the torqs, it wasn't always possible to evade them completely. This was especially true now with the crush of bodies and moving limbs crammed into the limited space.

Now that the last monster was past the barriers, it would be time to spring the trap. It would have been natural for Sadavir to worry about the plan at this point, to go over all the things that could go wrong. As it was, Sadavir couldn't spare a single thought for the plan or any element in it. He was being pushed to his limit trying to survive.

Some part of his mind still registered the change, however, when the cavern started growing darker and darker. The passages to the outside had provided some small beams of light, whatever could make it past the lanky beasts that mostly filled the tunnels.

Now even those small, fluttering beams were winking out. The tunnels were being closed from the outside, sealing the monsters into the mountain. One tunnel closed all by itself as the thrashing of the alpha caused a neighboring tunnel to cave in.

Sadavir's nimble acrobatics had dissolved into a frantic scrambling in the darkness. There were too many arms, bodies, and claws to dodge at this point. His only focus was to keep clear of the claws and somehow keep from being crushed against the wall. So his progress through the cave was more like a leaf caught in the rapids of a river, bouncing off of every obstacle, rolling and stumbling from one danger right into another.

Things actually got a little better as the last of the tunnels was sealed and the darkness was complete. Most of the creatures stopped trying to catch Sadavir and started trying to turn around to get back out of the tunnels, sensing they were trapped. Turning around was impossible, of course, and trying to move backward would never give them the power they would need to break through the tons of rock that now sealed their escape. The teams above hadn't bothered crafting fitted doors. It was far easier and faster to destroy portions of the tunnels and let them collapse under their own weight.

The alpha would not be turned from his bloodlust and continued swiping around in the darkness, though the beast was hitting his fellow monsters more often than not. Sadavir was able to use the confusion to his advantage and managed to rest a moment, crouched by the stone table that had served as his bed for weeks.

He could feel the rumbling in the rock all around him as the massive animals crashed and struggled. The very air vibrated against his skin as roars of panic, pain, and anger echoed through the tiny space.

He smiled in the darkness at his situation. It had been his idea to be here, of course, but he couldn't help but reflect on what a ridiculous idea it was. After all, sometimes traps worked and sometimes they didn't, but they nearly always turned out badly for the bait.

Luckily, there wasn't much left to do. Now that the tunnels were all closed, Sadavir looked upward. There! Across the cavern, a single beam of light formed like a glowing pillar in the swirling dust of the cavern. A rope lowered tentatively into the beam, like a shy snake poking its head from its hole.

The light gave Sadavir an instant picture of the contested territory he would have to cross to get to the rope. One of the smaller beasts was wounded and thrashing, cut by the claws of the alpha. The commotion only served to enrage the alpha more and it was busy swiping its claws in broad arcs over the area.

Sadavir shifted to the left, clear of his shelter. He took a deep breath, letting it out slowly while he rolled one shoulder, then the other. He didn't really need to limber up, rather, he was checking himself for any limited movement. He had learned that he didn't always notice wounds when he was in the full heat of battle. He was satisfied when his body responded easily to the rolling movements, none of the stiffness or twitching pain that might indicate a wound, pulled muscle, or broken bone.

With no further preparation, Sadavir leapt from his hiding place into a full sprint, reaching full speed within three steps. The alpha's arm was in the middle of a backswing when it stopped abruptly and switched direction. Some sense had alerted it to Sadavir's motion and it snatched at him, claws grasping.

Sadavir slid under the arm feet first, carving a groove in the soft floor of the cave. He pulled himself into a ball once he was under the arm, pulling his feet back under his body. Every muscle in his body tensed with the effort as he sprang from the ground.

He had made it to the wounded beast on the cave floor. It had been hit a few more times by the alpha and wasn't moving anymore. Sadavir's jump carried him over most of the monster, but not entirely. He planted both hands on the thing's chest and pushed hard. His momentum had carried his feet over him and now he sprang off his hands, pushing his feet into the air and over the claws that made a feeble grasp at him.

He brought his feet back under him in the air

and landed in a roll on the far side of the beast. Two more steps and a jump and his hand closed around the rope.

"PULL!" he screamed, his voice a lot more hoarse and frantic than he had intended. Luckily for him, the entire party had been waiting for any tug on the rope and the command was entirely unnecessary. They heaved on the rope and Sadavir shot through the opening like water escaping a geyser.

What felt like dozens of hands pulled him from the mouth of the small tunnel. Strong hands clapped him on the shoulder in congratulations. Gentler hands pushed and probed, checking for injury. Voices overlapped all around him, but he couldn't piece together any complete sentences. This was partially due to everyone talking at once, but mostly because of the pulsing ringing in his ears that was still dying down after the intense cacophony in the cave.

He let them guide him down the side of the hill. Someone pressed a flask of water into his hand and he raised it gratefully to his lips. He gagged on his first swallow, however, suddenly realizing the quantity of dirt and dust in his mouth. He coughed and spat out his first mouthful of muddy water and swished a second around before spitting that out as well.

Once his mouth was clean, he drank greedily from the flask, small streams of water escaping from the corners of his mouth to form muddy streaks in the dirt that caked his entire body. Finally, his ears cleared enough that Vova's voice made it through.

"I wish I could have seen that!" he crowed.

"There wasn't much to see," Sadavir rasped. He hadn't noticed at the time, but he realized now the rough treatment he had given his throat. Heavy athletics in an enclosed space with large bodies constantly churning dust into the air was a sure fire way to scratch things up.

Blinking his eyes clear, he stared around at a ring of smiling faces. No one was missing, no one was injured. Hope had returned.

# Chapter 17

The group continued to press him for stories as they walked back toward the open plain they had come from. It took a while before he could convince them that the sprawling scramble for survival, while exciting, didn't make for much of a narrative.

Everyone grew silent as they cleared the hills and stepped out onto the plains. The hulking carcass of the monster that had first hunted Sadavir lay sprawled out in the tall grasses.

The work of decomposition was well on its way and most of the party turned aside, holding their noses and trying not to breathe when the wind wafted the stench their way.

Sadavir, with Vova by his side, approached the dead body. It didn't look nearly as large with the muscles largely melted away or consumed by smaller scavengers. Still, the absurdly long claws looked bleached in the sun and stood out like long white swords leaning on a rack.

"Look at this," Vova beckoned Sadavir over to the head. Once Sadavir had joined him, Vova used a stick to push the decayed lips farther back from the teeth. Four long fangs, two on top and two on bottom, fit together perfectly, the motion of the jaw serving to sharpen them.

Sadavir shuddered involuntarily.

"Those things will haunt my dreams the rest of my life," he confessed to Vova. His friend looked sympathetic, but was already shaking his head.

"You're missing the point. There's something much scarier here than fangs. Look at the back."

Sadavir leaned over to get a closer look at the back of the thing's mouth. He looked for what had so concerned his friend, but the rest seemed fairly mundane. The back teeth were flat and worn. He looked back at Vova and shrugged his shoulders.

"Molars, Sadavir," Vova clarified. "Not sharp, tearing teeth for eating meat, these are flat, grinding teeth for eating plants."

He paused, waiting again for Sadavir to comprehend this new discovery. When all he got back was a blank stare, he sighed dramatically.

"May the powers save me from the Creators' education system," he remarked, rolling his eyes. "These creatures are omnivorous, meaning they can eat plants or animals. This matters because most predators are very limited in number due to how many prey animals are available."

"But if they don't need meat to survive..." Sadavir began.

"Then there is no effective limit to how many of

these things there might be. We've seen small packs, but if they can live off greens, there's no reason why there couldn't be entire herds up here."

"Herds..." Sadavir whispered the word. There were villages to the east of Surac that kept cattle. Sadavir had visited them once and had stood in awe of the vast number of animals that swept over the wide prairie. Now his mind boggled as he tried and failed to imagine replacing every plodding animal in that herd with one of these violent monsters.

"We'd better get back," both men spoke in unison, deeply unnerved by this new discovery and the possible implications. As horrific as their experience had been, there was a distinct possibility that they had been absurdly lucky thus far, only running into small numbers.

It was a sobering thought as they made their way back to the cliffs.

Luckily for Sadavir, one of the stone shapers in Vova's group, a tough middle-aged woman named Sandra, had a sharp eye for geography. While many of them had been running madly for their lives, Sadavir included, Sandra had kept a watchful eye on the surrounding terrain, picking out landmarks and gauging distances.

As a result, the return trip was much faster and smoother than the ragged journey to the hills. They still moved carefully, of course, but now that they knew what they were dealing with, they were able to scout much more effectively. They evaded any area that showed any sign at all of ravaged trees or the torn soil patterns that were caused by the large claws.

Sadavir was surprised and relieved when finally the landscape became familiar and the building site around the cliff came into view. His surprise at making it safely, however, was dwarfed entirely by his surprise at seeing a new structure standing by the cliff's edge.

Made entirely of steel, it formed a barrier of bars along the bottom. The edifice itself rose above everything else. Made with minimal steel, the thing looked flimsy and skeletal. Sadavir wasn't fooled, though. He recognized the reinforcing structure that made the tower much safer than it looked. After all, he had grown up training on a steel cage that looked just like it, made for him by his...

"Papa?" Sadavir called out as soon as they were within hearing distance. At the top of the tower, Aric's large, shaggy head poked out from behind a large contraption that sat on top of the tower like a setting hen.

"Sadavir!" Aric immediately started scrambling down the tower, which made it sway ever so slightly. Sadavir could have imagined it, but he thought he heard a groan come from the tower right where Aric left it.

Aric grabbed his son off the ground and held

him as if he were still a little boy, instead of a fully grown man in his mid twenties. Sadavir was too relieved to see his father to mind much, though he did hear some muffled snickers behind him.

"You found them!" Aric exclaimed, lowering his son back to the ground and looking over his shoulder at the ragged group of explorers.

"I found half of them," Sadavir admitted. "There's another group that left in the opposite direction, I haven't had a chance to look for them yet."

Aric shook his head in wonder.

"I can't believe they made it so far!" he exclaimed. "Considering how long it took you to reach them, they must have been to the far side of the world and back!"

Aric's eyes lit up with the prospect, already looking hungrily at the rest of the party, eager to hear the stories. Sadavir brought him back to reality with a jarring thud.

"They didn't make it very far at all. They were holed up in those hills off to the west there. We've spent the last few weeks trying to stay alive after running into massive bloodthirsty monsters that hunt us like we're no more than rabbits."

Aric's smile melted and drooped like a candle dropped into hot coals. With his initial bubble of enthusiasm popped, he now looked at the crowd of people and saw how many were missing. His bear-like
110

shoulders dropped.

"But surely you were able to..." he began, but Sadavir was already shaking his head and lifting his shirt to display the wandering, ragged scar left behind from his injury.

"I only ran into one and it nearly killed me. I wasn't able to fight it at all. All I could do was run."

The bitterness in Sadavir's tone threatened to overwhelm him. He had said these things before, but admitting it to his father held a special kind of sting.

Aric took another look at his son, peering as if trying to see into his soul. He had been hurt, that was for sure, but it went deeper than the physical wound. The answer came to Aric all at once.

Sadavir had never lost. He had been challenged, pushed, he had even failed on multiple occasions, but he had never truly lost. Now he had faced a violent death, been helpless to stop it, and had escaped only by luck and the brave efforts and sacrifice of others.

Aric had always thought of his son as the bravest of men. Now, in a rush, he realized what a glaring gap he had left in the boy's training. Sadavir hadn't truly learned how to deal with fear, that terror that pushed a person to give up and choose mediocrity or even death.

"What are you going to do?" Aric asked him quietly. He hoped it wasn't anything too stupid. Sadavir was still in pain from his experience, and men in pain make poor decisions. Still, there would be very little he could do to stop him at this point.

"Get these back down the cliff," Sadavir ordered. "I'm going to go and find the others."

"Do you think they're still alive?"

"I don't know. I'll be honest, I don't think their chances were very good. Still, I remember what it felt like to be hunted by these things. If our people aren't dead yet, then they are in serious trouble. I can't leave them behind."

Aric nodded. It wasn't the best decision, but it wasn't the worst, either. If nothing else, it was being done for the right reasons.

"Now what have you built here?" Sadavir asked, gesturing towards the tower and the odd contraption sitting on top of it.

"Do you like it?" Aric was back to grinning in a second. There were few things he enjoyed more in life than showing off his inventions.

"What is it?" Sadavir asked as the two of them walked back to take a closer look.

"I don't really have a name for it yet," Aric began. "We all knew there was something dangerous up here, we just didn't know what. The way I saw it, you might need some cover when you came back. So we built the bar cage around the scaffolding so that people could get onto it while being protected.

"Then I built the tower so I could see you coming and we could be prepared. Then, once I had the tower built..."

"Wait," Sadavir interrupted. "Where did you get the steel to build all this? I know there was a little here left over, but there couldn't have been that much. There certainly wasn't enough to build all this."

"Oh, that..." Aric looked suddenly embarrassed. "After a couple days, I decided it would be best if we..."

"Pillaged the bloody safety bars!" a new voice roared down from the tower. Sadavir couldn't even recognize the voice until another ragged figure started picking his way down the tower. Andre moved very carefully, but he continued yelling as he descended.

"It's not like the big oaf didn't know how hard it was in the first place coming up here! Then I finally get solid ground under my feet again for a couple days and what does he do?"

Andre finally got both feet on the ground and started stalking his way toward Aric.

"He tells me we have to go back out onto the scaffolding! And not to go home, as good sense would suggest. No! That would be too logical for your father. Instead, he wants my help harvesting what he called 'non-essential' bars from the scaffolding.

"Do you know what he considered 'non-essential'? Any bar that existed to keep you from falling to your doom! That's where he got his precious steel!"

Sadavir threw his arms around the raving man and hugged him tight. Andre returned the embrace without stopping his complaining.

"Andre! How did my dad convince you to come up here?"

Andre leveled a baleful glare at the blacksmith.

"Blackmail! He threatened slander of the worst kind, Sadavir. That's how your dear father got his former best friend to come with him on this fool's errand. He threatened to tell my wife that I chickened out."

"That would do it," Sadavir nodded along in mock gravity. He could tell that Andre was genuinely upset, but not so upset that his characteristic sense of humor had abandoned him. There was no real edge to his accusations.

"So why were you hiding up there?" Sadavir asked.

"Hiding? Being held captive is more like it. Apparently your father likes heights so much he insisted on building more of them as soon as we got here. He insists that we both stay up there as much as possible, even if one person leaves, so the other can man the weapon if there's trouble."

"What weapon? That thing at the top of the tower?"

"Yes," Andre confirmed. "That thing is a weapon meant to cover your retreat if you needed it. I came

114

down because I could tell that your father was about to take credit for inventing it."

"It was partly my idea," Aric huffed. Andre scoffed.

"No, your idea was to build a really big version of your launcher, even though you know the Stone-crafted steel doesn't have enough spring for that. My idea was much better."

Aric only hmphed in response.

"So how does it work?" Sadavir interjected, knowing it was the one subject that would distract them both equally.

They excitedly led him over to the tower and up to the weapon. A rack of weights hung from the bottom of the weapon, each attached to a different part of a wheel. The wheel, in turn, was attached to a couple throwing arms with a steel box at the end of each arm. Another box stood behind and slightly higher than the rest of the invention.

"This bar here decides how many weights will be released," Andre pointed out a bar that could be slid through each weight, keeping it from falling. "That way, we'd be able to have it throw at different distances."

"This bin here has a latch that allows us to fill the throwing arm with rocks with a single throw of the lever." Aric jumped in on the explanation, not wanting to be left out of the fun. "With the rapid loader mechanism, we've been able to fire it every three seconds until the weights hit the ground and have to be winched back up."

"And what is it firing?" Sadavir queried. Aric answered by pulling the lever on the feeding mechanism. A smaller bin rotated out of the larger one, dumping a predetermined amount of fist-sized rocks into the throwing arm bucket.

"And here's the best part!" Andre was too excited to even pretend to be mad at Aric as he pulled up a small lever and the entire weapon turned smoothly around its base. The entire thing was set into a circular track that allowed the men to aim it wherever they wanted to before firing.

Andre used this feature now to point the weapon away from the rest of the party, who had gathered just below the tower to see what was going on. Aric pulled the control rod back from three of the weights and Sadavir could see the tension on the wheel, waiting to be released.

Andre and Aric stepped to either side of the weapon with an ease that spoke of repeated practice. Then Aric stomped on one last lever on the floor and the weights dropped, spinning the throwing arm until it came to a jarring stop at the zenith of its arcing path. Everyone in the party jumped, startled by the unexpected loudness of steel hitting steel. The rocks inside the basket flew out a good thirty yards, landing and rolling harmlessly on the ground.

Sadavir laughed, in spite of all he'd been

through, to see the pride on the faces of the two older men. He clapped their shoulders and told them how impressive it was. After a sufficient amount of beaming, Aric lowered his eyes.

"When we built it, we imagined you being chased by groups of men, savages or some such, or perhaps wild animals. I fear this wouldn't mean much against the beasts you describe. Are they really that big?"

Sadavir nodded grimly.

"The smallest of them is as big as a house and stronger than a team of oxen. They have long arms and long legs that give them something of a gangly look, but the claws on the ends of their hands and feet are as long as swords and just as sharp.

"As things sit now, I don't see any way of fighting them. We need to get everyone away from this place."

"When will you go after the others?" Andre asked, jumping back into the conversation.

"Right now," Sadavir responded. "There's nothing to gain by waiting."

"Well, let's get down, then," Aric suggested. "The others are looking impatient."

# Chapter 18

When they rejoined the others at the base of the tower, Aric held back and watched Sadavir. At first, he smiled to himself as he saw his son's dedication as he jumped into the latest task. It was good to see that his trials up here hadn't affected his focus. That focus would bring him through anything.

After a couple minutes, Aric stopped smiling. Yes, Sadavir was as focused and energetic as ever, even more so, in fact. But something had changed. Aric's expressive face slowly moved from concern to a frown as he listened to Sadavir's string of commands issued to the survivors.

"No, leave that."

"I need three more packs of dried meat. You! Those two."

"There's nothing we can do about that and now is not the time to discuss it."

"Enough. Stop."

Sadavir snapped out each order with an air of impatience and irritation. Once Aric was aware of it, he noticed other small things that were even more concerning.

Sadavir wasn't using people's names. He had been with these people for weeks now, they had nursed him back to health and traveled through the wilderness together. Aric would have expected a strong bond formed between them. Instead, Sadavir pointed and barked like an angry schoolteacher.

Even more telling was that people weren't challenging the orders. Most of the people were older and more experienced than Sadavir. In many instances, Sadavir was telling them to do things that they had already done or they were already doing something better. Nobody argued or pointed out the flaws in what he was telling them to do. They obeyed.

Aric knew that people didn't suddenly turn submissive because of a single event. He was seeing the final effect of an ongoing pattern. Rather than bonding with these people, Sadavir had separated himself from them.

Aric had seen during their first conversation the small cracks fear had made in Sadavir. Now he realized how deeply those cracks ran. If his son wasn't careful, he'd shatter.

Sadavir drew a deep breath and let it out slowly as the first of the party disappeared over the edge of the cliff. They traveled light, most of the packs and provisions were being left behind. They would be home soon.

Each of them had taken a moment to thank him

before they left. He had nodded and thanked them in turn. He knew their gratitude was sincere, but it rang hollow in his own mind. He had done very little to help them at all. If anything, they had rescued him. Vova's quick thinking and Sandra's cool nerves had done more to save the party than Sadavir's acrobatics and paltry armbands.

In fact, in many ways, he felt like the original reasons he had for coming were no longer valid. All had agreed that he was the best one for the job because of his amazing defensive skills. But up here, they counted for nearly nothing. Never before had he felt so vulnerable, so ordinary.

He shook his head to clear his thoughts. Such musings had been weighing on him since the night of the first attack. Still, for all his doubts, the lessons of his childhood ran deep. He was a protector. This one fact was so deeply etched into his being he couldn't imagine who he would be without it.

So regardless of whether he was the best person for the job, he would do it.


Two packs rested by Sadavir's feet. They were full, the best of the remaining provisions gathered from all the other packs. One was for him, of course. The other belonged to Vova.

There had never been a discussion. Vova had quietly assembled a pack of his own as Sadavir had gotten everyone else in line and on their way. Sadavir saw what he was doing and there were several times when he could have stopped his friend, told him to go home. When each moment came, Sadavir couldn't bring himself to do it.

He would die before he admitted it, but his heart beat faster and cold sweat broke out on his back every time he glanced towards the forest he'd be walking into. His honor screamed at him that it was wrong to bring Vova. There would be no advantage to having another person along. Sadavir would be risking Vova's life so that he wouldn't have to be alone in that forest, like a child huddling close to his parents when it grew dark.

He felt disgusted with himself, his cowardice, but still he said nothing. Now people were leaving and Vova wasn't going with them. The last of the party went over the edge and Sadavir turned to Vova. Aric was leaned over, speaking quietly to the smaller man. Andre stood next to both of them, but managed to look completely disconnected from the conversation.

Sadavir marched over and interrupted.

"I appreciate the two of you coming up here, but there's nothing more you can do. Head back down the scaffolding and help the party if they need it."

Aric turned to Andre.

"I do believe he's mistaken me for someone else. Understandable, really, what with all the beating and running he's been through."

Andre nodded sagely, going along with the farce.

"Indeed, it's like he doesn't know you at all. Perhaps one of these great beasties knocked him about the head. Why, I knew one fellow took a blow to the head and didn't recognize his own wife for a full year. Luckily, she was the type didn't really mind reminding him on a daily basis."

"You don't say? I don't have that kind of patience. Maybe I can get by on one reminder if I make it strong enough," Aric said to Andre. Then turning to square up to Sadavir, he raised himself to his full height. Aric had the habit of leaning over a little when talking to people shorter than him, which was everyone. Now his back straightened and his shoulders rolled back, accentuating a torso shaped like a sturdy barrel. While Sadavir was very strong in his own right, he had only grown to average height and a wiry build. Aric's towering height and bull-like stature dwarfed him in every way.

"Sadavir," he rumbled. "I am your father. I am not your subject, your soldier, or even your friend. So the day you decide that you can order me around is the day I take your armbands away and send you home to your mother. Do I make myself clear?"

"Umm...yes, you do," Sadavir mumbled in response. He couldn't think of any of response. There was some small part of Sadavir's brain that wanted to puff his chest and argue with Aric. After all,

122

Sadavir was about to become a father himself. Wasn't it about time he wasn't treated like a child?

Luckily, the ruling part of his brain acknowledged that this was neither the time nor place to have a meaningless showdown with his father. Besides, he did suddenly feel a little silly ordering people around.

It was amazing to him how easily he had become accustomed to people obeying him. It was the kind of thing that snuck up on a person. Perhaps he should feel grateful to his father for keeping him grounded. It was a thought to be turned over at a later date.

"Vova, we should go over our plan." Anxious to shift the attention away from his father's scolding, Sadavir opted for an abrupt change of subject. Knowing that Sadavir would prefer to talk it over with Vova alone, Andre and Aric shifted meaningfully to include themselves in the conversation.

"I figure we head out in the direction they started and try to pick up their trail. You're a better tracker than I am, so..."

"Or..." Andre interrupted. "You could realize that unless they were chopping and burning trees along the way, you aren't going to find a month-old trail. Tracking involves looking for turned stones, bent grass, that sort of thing. The grass you see out there now could have been seeds when they passed by."

Sadavir grit his teeth hard enough that he could

hear them creak. He was used to Andre's sharp wit, he was always making fun of something or another. But now Sadavir found it humiliating. He turned to look at the man and the smile on Andre's face disappeared.

"Then what do you suggest?" Sadavir felt that he had asked the question politely, but Andre shifted backward slightly.

"I didn't mean anything by it." Andre defended himself. "I'm only saying that you'd have a better chance tracking those big things. I believe we're calling them torqs, right? From your stories, it sounds like you'd be able to follow claw marks that deep weeks after they had passed, not to mention the damage they'd do to the trees."

"Why would we track a torq?" Sadavir remained squared up to Andre and Andre remained on the defensive.

"It stands to reason that the missing party ran into one. Otherwise, they would be here by now. So that torq will have followed them. You can follow that trail until you find where it..."

Andre paused, trying to be delicate in his wording. Sadavir cut through his hesitation.

"We could follow it to where it killed them, you mean. No, don't apologize, there's no need to lie to ourselves. We all know it's a possibility. It's a good idea. Even if they're alive, the trail would lead us to clues as to how they survived. These things are obsessive in a hunt. If the party is alive, then we should be able to figure out how they fooled the torq, like when I found the tree burrows that Vova's team made."

Andre sighed, relieved that the discussion hadn't turned into more of an argument.

"We'll stay here." Aric filled in. "Andre and I can't move as quickly as you young people. We'll try to adjust our defenses here. We'll also be ready if you bring any wounded back. Olya sent me with herbs she said would help with bleeding or to fight off infection."

Andre watched Sadavir carefully. He had flinched or shivered slightly when Aric mentioned the herbs. It was a small thing, but Andre knew the importance of small things.

"Yes, that's good. Stay close to the edge so you can escape. You should hear these things coming well before they break the tree line. That will give you plenty of time to get down and out of the way," Sadavir said, already turning back to the packs.

"Don't worry, I'll look after him." Vova whispered to Aric, then turned to follow Sadavir, who had already scooped up his pack and was headed towards the tree line. He didn't say goodbye and he didn't look back.

# Chapter 19

"Could you believe that?" Aric asked Andre. "Whatever he's been through up here, it's getting to him."

Andre nodded. "I'll be honest with you, old friend, that put chills down my spine. A man as powerful as your son should never lose his sense of humor. That's how tyrants are born."

Aric scowled at him, but he looked more worried than irritated. An hour earlier, he would have argued furiously, called his friend crazy and a fear-monger. But he too had seen his son's attitude, the way he had treated people.

"There's nothing we can do about it now. We can only hope that he's not pushed much further."

"And what are the chances of that?" Andre scoffed. "It's a miracle this party survived. How do you think finding the other party dead is going to influence his world view? He's taking too much onto himself. All that responsibility is going to twist him with its weight."

"There's nothing for it now." Aric set his jaw. "You know, maybe it would be a good idea if you went with them after all. It looked like they could use all the help they could get. I don't think anything we'll get done up here will matter much if one of those torqs comes through here."

"So you're going to try the same thing your son did?" Andre bristled. "I'm as capable as you, you old tinsmith. If you're staying, then I'm staying. You're going to need me if we need to build something. Or what if Sadavir gets back and he..."

Andre froze, his sentence hanging like a broken branch in the air.

"The herbs..." he whispered to himself, offering no explanation. Aric waited for a long awkward pause for his friend to snap out of it. Andre snapped back in as fast as he had snapped out, but returned a completely different person.

He clapped Aric on the shoulder.

"You know what? You're right! I don't belong up here. I really should listen to you more often. Nadya always says you're a steadying influence on me. Or at least she suggests I spend more time at your house, anyway.

"So I'll bow to your wisdom on this one. It's time I got back."

Andre turned and started to walk away, directly towards the edge of the cliff where the scaffolding awaited.

"Wait!" Aric called after him, baffled. "You're going now?"

"Yup! No time like the present, as you always say!"

"I don't say that, you do! And you don't even have a pack."

Andre didn't miss a beat and scooped one of the abandoned packs off the ground and swung it over his shoulder without checking its contents. He was nearly to the scaffolding.

"Are you even going to help the other people get down?" Aric was incredulous.

"Nope! They seem like good, stout young folk. They've made it this far, I'm sure it would only rob them of their sense of victory if I helped them now."

Andre's feet were already on the scaffolding and his head bobbed as it got lower and lower.

"I'll say hello to everybody for you, ok? Take care of yourself, Aric!"

And then he was gone. Only the light repetitive clang of shoes on metal marked his swift descent down the scaffolding.

*Andre had a plan,* Aric told himself. That was the only thing that made any sense at all. Andre liked to whine so that people would appreciate his efforts, but he never actually shrank from a duty. His sudden and swift departure was as out of character as his gentle Sadavir turning dark and bossing everyone around. Andre had a plan, he told himself again.

Or maybe the whole world was going crazy.

*******

Vova gave them their beginning direction. He had been there when the parties had parted ways. The two groups had discussed their intended directions, and Vova had even stood and watched as the other crew left before leading his own team into the unknown.

In spite of Andre's negativity about the subject, Vova was able to find blackened wood from the party's first night's fire later that afternoon. The following morning, they found trees that had branches cut off with metal blades. Rather than moving stealthily through the forest, the party seemed to have hacked and slashed their way through the trees. Still, Andre had a point, after a month, even deep signs could only be recognized faintly.

The two men had packed lightly were moving much faster than the full party had been able to. This party had had more builders and they had lugged more materials, especially metal, into the wilderness with them. They knew they would need tools and other equipment if they wanted to build an outpost up here at some point. Preparation and ambition had been chosen over speed.

Besides that, Sadavir and Vova also had an urgency driving them. They moved quickly and quietly, never speaking above a whisper. They knew

129

now that this land would not be claimed. They were strangers here and if discovered, would be snuffed out as quickly as flies.

They camped cold and silent, wrapping themselves in their cloaks, sleeping apart and tucked under whatever roots or overhanging earth they could manage to drag onto themselves.

They only found one more campfire traveling in a straight line. After traveling nearly a day with no more clear signs, they decided to change tactics.

The two ranged outward, moving in expanding circles until one of them found some sign, then he would signal to the other, they would converge on the spot, and the process would start over. It was slow going, but still better than getting lost. The hack and slash tactics had changed abruptly and they had a harder time finding anything like a trail.

It was because of the fading trail that they had reason to hope. The careful movement suggested that this party had somehow discovered the beasts without being first discovered themselves. Having time to move and prepare would have given them a great advantage in survival. They traveled feeling grateful each time they found a small trace of the party's passing, rather than a scene of carnage and scattered supplies.

On the third day, Andre's prediction came true. They found markings from one of the massive torqs. Its trail of broken branches and gouged soil could have been followed by a blind man. And it followed nearly a straight line, headed in the same direction the party had last been pointed. It was the path of a hunter, tracking prey. If it had been grazing for foliage, it would have meandered in random directions.

The two exchanged looks, but no conversation was needed. They had an easy path now, but every step would bring them closer to a hunting torq. It turned out to be a fairly short path.

On the third day, Sadavir and Vova came to the edge of the trees and stopped dead in their tracks. The minutes passed unnoticed as the two men processed what they were seeing.

It was as if a giant hand had swept the land clean. Trees and grasses were consumed or trampled into dust for what looked like miles. Writhing crowds of the monsters pulsed and throbbed as they wandered around, fought amongst themselves, or simply stretched out and napped in the uninterrupted sunshine.

It had the look of a vast circle, with the greatest amount of activity happening at the center. There, beasts roared and hammered at something. Occasionally, their rage would erupt and two lesser males would slash at each other over some perceived challenge.

"Have we found them?" Vova whispered. "Is that what they're fighting over? The trail was leading here."

"I know," Sadavir whispered back. "It's possible they managed to take cover there in the center. Still, I could never have imagined a group this big. There must be hundreds! And look at this place, they must have been here for weeks to do this much damage to all these trees. Could they have survived this long?"

"Could we really leave them here without knowing?" Vova softly rebuked him. Sadavir shook his head grimly.

"Of course not. I wouldn't leave my worst enemy to such a fate. But how will we get past them to check? We couldn't effectively battle one of these things. This is a horde."

"Well, we know they're simple-minded. Maybe we can lure them away."

The two friends stood at the edge of the clearing and watched, looking for patterns, opportunities, and possible openings. Then they retreated further back into the woods where they could talk, plan, and argue more freely. Finally, they came to an agreement.

It was impossible.

# Chapter 20

It was a dark conclusion, but inevitable. There was simply no way to attract the attention of the beasts that wouldn't make their own scent the new target. They lacked the team and resources to either run away or defend themselves against a group of this size. Still, they were resolved not to give up.

"Maybe we're underestimating them," Sadavir suggested. "After all, these were our best people, and they had more time to prepare. Maybe we don't need to figure out every part of the escape plan here. They must have thought of something, we only need to figure out what their plan is and how we can help. Maybe they're trying to tunnel out even now, like we did."

It was a foolish bit of hope, but it was the best that either of them could come up with. They worked their way around the outside of the circle, keeping to the trees. It took them most of the day, as they moved slowly and carefully, only moving from one cover to another when they'd sat and watched a while, making sure they weren't walking into an ambush. They'd made it halfway around the circle when Sadavir saw something on a low tree branch.

It was a thread. It was the kind of thing that would have happened on accident, a stray bit of fluff that caught on the point of a branch. But that little wisp of textile told Sadavir volumes. He waved Vova over, pointed, and whispered urgently.

"They passed by here." He stared at Vova while he waited for the other man to put the pieces together. To Vova's credit, it didn't take him long. They were halfway across the circle, almost on the exact same path they had left in the first place. There was little chance that the party would have made it this far, then backtracked just to be pinned down.

"I think they had the same idea," Vova whispered. "They created a distraction. That's what's back there."

Sadavir nodded his agreement and the two gratefully moved farther down the path, putting welcome distance between them and the vast herd of monsters.

They found the second distraction that evening.

They smelled it before they saw it. The putrid stench of rotting flesh hit their nostrils like a chemical attack. They gagged and worked their way upwind before approaching the buried cage.

It looked a little like an enormous crouched porcupine. Crafted metal bars protected a device and a pile of small dead animals a couple feet under the ground. Covering the top of the cage were vicious metal spikes jutting out in all directions.

Most curious of all, at the exact center of the cage, there was a contraption that looked to have a freely swinging arm, with heavy weights set off to each side.

"It almost looks like one of my father's inventions. He and a couple others have been working on something similar to keep track of time," Sadavir commented. "Look at those counterweights, there. This device is supposed to move, rocking back and forth on that track there. At each side, it would strike against those metal plates. It would make quite a racket."

"That would certainly drive those creatures insane trying to get to it. So why isn't it working?"

Sadavir shook his head absentmindedly, moving around the cage. Then he spotted it.

"There!" he pointed triumphantly. "The pile of animals shifted and one of them fell off, a bit of foot is on the track. That would have slowed down the motion faster. I'll bet it only ran for a day or so before stopping."

"So how long is it supposed to run?" Vova asked. Sadavir didn't miss the grave tone. If there was a device like this keeping that enormous herd gathered, then it could only be a matter of time before it also ran out.

"I don't know," Sadavir admitted. "Inventions are my father's strength, not mine. His very best time-keeping inventions only last a few days before needing the counter balances and springs reset."

"So even if there's someone up here who's a better inventor than your father, there's still a very good chance that that herd will be breaking up soon. Rotting meat won't hold them forever. Then they're going to be hunting us."

Sadavir nodded and neither of them spoke as they thought through the magnitude of their problem. A herd that large would diffuse out in all directions. Inevitably, they would cross the trail of the people who left. Or, they realized almost simultaneously, the creatures would discover Sadavir and Vova's own trail, as they had crossed too near to the main herd while scouting.

"Let's move," Sadavir suggested, disappointed in himself that he wasn't fully able to keep the panic from his voice. "Speed is our only hope, we've got to find them and get back before the torqs start tracking us."

Mentally, they drew a line from the center of the large herd to this device. It stood to reason that the other group would continue traveling in the same direction, headed in a diagonal path towards the cliffs.

They ate and drank on the move, neither of them daring to waste even a minute to rest. If anything, they started walking faster as the day wore on, even jogging when the terrain was smooth. They were like two children walking home in the darkness, trying to be brave for one another, but still getting more and more scared with each movement from the shadows.

Luck favored them and only a day and a half after leaving the torq horde, they saw the wispy smoke of a campfire in the distance. They covered the last few hundred meters at a full run. The survivors met them coming the opposite direction, equally as thrilled to see the small rescue party.

They had, indeed, fared better than Vova's party or Sadavir himself. This was a prepared camp, not huddling survivors. A tall tower held a lookout who was still actively scanning the trees behind Sadavir and Vova. Ironically, the watchman had been so intent on looking for the hulking beasts that he had, at first, missed the rescue party creeping through the thick forest until they were fully in the clear.

Long sharp spikes, looking like they'd been crafted from whole trees, stuck out at an angle from the ground, outward from the camp on all sides. Rather than finishing each tree into a single spike, they had sharpened the branches as well, creating a random mess of sharp points that leaned upon one another, helping to support the structure, as well as make it even more difficult for a large creature to get past.

A closer look at the camp showed even more preparations. Their food was equally portioned out in packs kept at steady intervals around the camp. If an attack came and they lost some supplies, most of them would be able to grab a pack and scatter.

Tunnels had already been carved into the rock, giving quick escape routes should the outer defenses be breached.

Sadavir and Vova squeezed themselves through the lower openings of the poles, accompanied by excited explorers.

For several minutes, questions and answers flew like volleys of arrows back and forth. Information gushed out from both sides in breathless rushes in between returning questions.

Others had survived.

No one from this group had been killed yet.

Sadavir had come up to find them.

This group had been using their crafting to make diversions and tunnels, though they had been fully cut off from returning back the way they had come.

A quick list of names brought grief and shock as Vova related who among his party had fallen to the torqs.

This group was making a new way back down.

At that last revelation, Sadavir waved aside all other questions and even cut someone else off who was describing how they'd set up their defenses.

"You're making another way down?" Sadavir pressed, focusing in on the person who had brought it up. There wasn't a clear leader in this group. Rather, a group of three had created a kind of team leadership. It was to one of these that Sadavir directed his questions. "How are you doing that? It took us a long time and a tremendous amount of iron to craft the scaffolding."

"You Creators always think of building as the only answer," the person chided, though she smiled as she did it, showing that there was no ill will. "Sometimes you can make something faster by destroying what you don't need."

"We have three teams worth of light blue Stones. The Destroyers have been working in shifts to carve out switchbacks heading down the cliff face."

"That's sharp thinking," Vova said, nodding in approval. "Sadavir, we can get down to the valley floor, then climb up the scaffolding to let the others know we're safe, we don't have to go back by that enormous herd at all!"

For the first time in a long time, Sadavir smiled. Maybe no one else needed to die.

# Chapter 21

They spent a quiet night there with the other team. The longer Sadavir spent with them, the more he relaxed. After his first encounter with the torqs, he had only expected to find bodies, blood, and fear up in this vast and terrible land. Now, sitting around the fire and telling stories with healthy people who had managed to stay a step ahead of the things, hope had returned in full.

The only breaks in the evening were the shift changes for the Stone teams who were working on the way down, as well as people changing out for guard duty. Sadavir and Vova insisted on taking their turns in the guard tower, in spite of their long and grueling journey to find them.

Once he had finished his guard duty shift, Sadavir rolled up in his blankets and slept until the sun was full in the sky. Nightmares only woke him twice.

It was boredom that drove him to go down and inspect the switchbacks on the afternoon of the second day. He had a strong bias for action, and while there was nothing he could do to help, he still took the time to scale down to where they worked, if only to offer encouragement.

It was a little surprising and disorienting at first to find that the tunneling left one side open. Sadavir didn't consider himself afraid of heights at all, but he did find it easier to make his way down the tunnel if he kept his eyes on the floor or the wall. Seeing so much open space stretched out into nothing and only a single step away from a deadly drop would have been enough to intimidate any man, woman, or child. Sadavir, for all his bravery, simply wasn't an exception.

He asked about the bizarre design choice as soon as he reached the workers. Really, it was only one worker. The Destroyer held both light blue Stones, both the opaque and the clear. He held both out towards the rock as it disintegrated under the pale glow of the light. Sadavir took a moment to marvel, though he had seen it many times before. Warm lines of light pulsed down the man's arm and coalesced into jagged lines of light over his fist. The pale blue color made it seem as if the man had managed to grab a messy handful of bright blue summer sky.

The Creator sat well behind his partner, clearly bored, but still intent. The people had experimented with every possible configuration, but at the end of the day, working with the Stones took both Creator and Destroyer. While just one could hold both Stones and direct the power, it would only work if the owner of the other Stone was also lending their concentration and strength.

The effect weakened with distance. Only Sadavir and Olya had managed to get their Stones to operate at over a hundred paces. For most people, the range was considerably lower. In this situation, where speed was critical, the Creator would stay very close to lend as much strength as possible.

So it was that the sitting man answered Sadavir's question about the open side with a distracted tone.

"For several reasons, really. First of all, it saves us a little bit of cutting. It might not be much, but even a little can add up when it's this large of a project. Secondly, we didn't dare bring fire into a closed tunnel for fear that we might smoke ourselves out, so we figured we'd at least want to leave some of it open for light. Otherwise we'd be tripping over each other in the dark.

"Lastly," the man smiled absently at this last tidbit of information, "we've only got one member of the party who's afraid of heights, which makes sense when you figure they had to volunteer to come up the scaffolding in the first place. But we've got three people in our party who have an abiding fear of enclosed spaces."

"Makes sense," Sadavir nodded along.

"You get used to it after a while," the man

continued, clearly happy to have someone to talk to, even if it was only with a fraction of his attention. "And it's not like we needed to set up anything fancy. We'll only be using this thing once."

"That's certainly true," Sadavir chuckled. "I certainly never intend to..."

He cut himself off. Something pinged his instincts and he went completely still.

He must have visibly tensed, because the man he'd been talking to also went still, looking at him. That, in turn, broke his concentration and the work on the tunnel stopped abruptly.

In that moment of silence, a clear sound confirmed what Sadavir's instincts had suggested. A scream.

Sadavir started to move, but the man nearest him grabbed his arm.

"You won't be able to make it up there in time to do anything. They'll escape down into the holes we have ready."

Sadavir shook the hand free and started his frantic climb back up, taking a moment to shout back over his shoulder.

"And then what?"

He felt more angry with each step, first angry at the torqs, then angry at himself. He had let himself get complacent, let himself believe that others had made sufficient preparations. Now people were dying again because of his weakness.

He had only made it about halfway to the top of the cliff when he stopped suddenly, pinning himself against the inner wall as a hail of pebbles and broken rock rained down next to him. After the initial rush, he poked his head out to see what had caused the sudden miniature landslide.

His stomach twisted and a sudden nausea swept over him as he saw the massive legs of a torq finding footholds as it worked its way down the cliff face. It moved with surprising ease, unconcerned with the immensity of the drop behind it. The long claws on feet and hands clung easily to the new openings in the rock and the thing scaled down the cliff faster that Sadavir could have made it down the tunnel.

Why would it...? Sadavir started to question the torq's behavior, but the answer came to him all at once. The thing was tracking him. That could only mean that it had crossed the path that he and Vova had made coming this way. With any luck, Vova had made it into one of the tunnels.

Now the thing was climbing right down the cliff face to get at Sadavir. A few glistening drops of blood glistened as they shot past him. The beast had been wounded by the defenses around the camp, but it hadn't been enough to stop it.

Sadavir's legs felt as heavy as stone, anchored into this endless cliff by fear and despair. These demonic beasts never stopped. A part of his brain raged against the unnatural, determined bloodlust of these creatures. But for all his anger, he couldn't move his feet.

He couldn't fight this. His armbands, hanging useless at his sides, meant nothing in this environment. The only movements he had available to him were to climb farther down, which would only mean leading the beast to the other two helpless men below, or climb higher, which would only serve to end the whole charade sooner.

The fear Sadavir had been holding in and working through for weeks now burst free, burning at his mind like molten iron. His strong, callused hands quivered and his brave face and strong jaw only supported panicked eyes and quivering lips. Tears sprung to his eyes as he thought suddenly of his mother.

Stone crunched nearby. So incredibly close now.

His mind stopped analyzing options, stopped looking for solutions. Instead, it played through what seemed like thousands of scenarios of death and pain. Each one seemed as real as if the claws were already ripping into him and his body jerked as if already stabbed.

In the midst of his meltdown into fear, he saw Vova's face. It was only there for an instant, looking almost serene.

It took Sadavir one endlessly long minute to realize that his friend's face hadn't been a hallucination. It was the silence that ultimately made the reality sink in.

The torq was gone, there were no more scratching and grinding noises of the descending beast. And he really had seen his friend's face for one fraction of an instant.

His numb mind nudged the puzzle pieces together grudgingly. Vova had seen the torq climbing down and had jumped down onto it, breaking it free of the wall to fall to its death.

The fear was gone suddenly, taking the stiffness with it. Sadavir slumped to his knees. The small tunnel and the open side meant that doing so placed his knees even with the cliff face. He felt updrafts of warm air rush by his face. In this stance, if he leaned over to look down where Vova and the torq had fallen, he would tip and fall himself.

Sadavir's mind tried to accept the reality of Vova's death and sacrifice, but it wouldn't take hold. There should have been a battle at the end of such a life. Vova should have perished from his wounds, surrounded by fallen enemies and mourned by close friends and family. The quiet drop through nothingness was too anticlimactic.

No speech. No fanfare. No heroic moment of decision. Not even a defiant yell from Vova or a death scream from the torq.

Only a moment of sacrifice and a dear friend reduced to nothing more than a dropped weight.

# Chapter 22

Sadavir knelt there until the men from below joined him in their feverish efforts to get back up to the top. Though he moved quickly in front of them, the path was only wide enough for one person at a time and barely that. He still felt as if he were moving through water. Everything was dimmed and moved slowly.

When he reached the top, he found feverish activity. Men scrambled to reassemble their defenses, which had been crushed onto both sides of a massive gap. It looked like a giant bull pushing his way through reeds by a riverbank.

Their arrival topside threw everyone into an even higher frenzy. They ignored Sadavir initially, turning their attention on the team that had been tunneling. They gestured and yelled furiously. They needed more speed than ever now, the two men should be down there, working for all they were worth. A second team would join them and try to add their own strength...

"No."

Sadavir spoke softly. Either no one heard, or no

one cared.

"NO!" he roared. Those closest to him staggered backward, startled by the extreme outburst. Even those on the outskirts of the camp trying to repair the wooden structure dropped what they were doing and turned to look at Sadavir.

Those closest took an extra step back that had nothing to do with being startled. Dark light had started to ripple across the surface of Sadavir's Stone, which he still wore around his neck in the Creator style. Not only were his fists clenched and knuckles white, even the placement of his feet and the bend of his knees spoke of a man ready for immediate violence.

"We're leaving, and we're leaving now," he growled. His chest heaved as if from heavy exertion, though no sweat beaded on his brow. "Grab what you can and follow me."

"But the way down! We're so close!" one of the men protested. Sadavir crossed the space between them in less time than it took the man to blink. A single-handed shove at the end of his momentum was all it took to toss the unprepared man to the ground.

Sadavir loomed over him, the sound of his teeth grinding together the only sound for two whole breaths.

"You're not close," the darkness in his voice bordered on contempt. "And that is the only positive thing left in this fiasco. Your tunnel still ends high enough right now that a fall would be deadly. And it will stay that way, because I will kill any man who tries to extend it even a hair's breadth farther."

He turned his head, making eye contact with every single one of the party who bore light blue Stones. Each one cringed under his gaze. They saw their own mortality in those eyes. None doubted he would kill them, and everyone knew he could.

"Why?" a woman behind him choked on the word, taking in another halting breath through the nose before she continued. "Would you have us die up here? Have you..."

She swallowed whatever she had been going to say and took another step backward as Sadavir focused in on her.

"Yes. I would let all of us die up here," he started. "That would be better than letting those things down the cliff and into our homeland. That thing was able to climb down using your tunnel as easy as I climb a ladder. We let our own selfish desires blind us to what we could have unleashed on our families back home."

"What if we went deeper from now on?" one of the light blue Stones offered the question timidly, almost apologetically. "We could burrow directly into the rock now, we could even hollow out caves in the rock for people to stay in so they don't have to stay up here. There's not much need to keep watch now we know they're coming for us."

"Not good enough," Sadavir snapped. He was only getting more enraged by the discussion. A growing part of him raged at even having to explain himself. "I'm going to need all of you to get back to the scaffolding alive."

He stared back at their uncomprehending eyes and hated them in that moment. It was irrational and it passed quickly, but he hated them. Hated them for letting Vova die, hated them for building a way for the torqs to make it down the cliff, and hated them most of all for the fact that, when it had mattered, he had been as bad as any of them.

That understanding of his own weakness and faults had not brought empathy, but increased rage as he reflected his own internal anguish out onto them like spewing acid.

"If they can climb down holes we made in the rock face," he explained as if to children, "they can climb down the scaffolding. We need to get back there and take it apart as we go down. This one was likely a straggler, but it shows that the full herd is breaking up and will be crossing our scent trail.

"Some might come this way, hunting us here. But it's certain that at least a few will start wandering down our back trail, and that will lead them right to the scaffolding and our homes. So yes, I need everyone, and yes, I am willing to spend your lives to get back there as fast as I can. Have I made myself clear now?"

Heads around the camp nodded.

"Do any intend to oppose me?"

Heads shook, but slower and more sullenly. These were good people. They would have agreed to the sacrifice if they'd been brought around to knowing that was the choice they faced. Now they had been forced into it. It was still the right choice, but it surely rankled.

Still, not a single foot dragged. The decision had been made and they were committed. They stuffed supplies into bags, scrambling from place to place in an inefficient bustle. What couldn't be packed quickly was left behind, which was most of everything, except for food. Without being told, they knew that they would be traveling too quickly to forage food from the land.

They abandoned previous paths and made their trip back hugging the cliff's edge. This served the dual purpose of keeping them as far as possible from the main herd, and making sure they didn't get lost. They would be moving quickly, and often in the dark. Though it did force them to extra caution making sure none of them fell off, all of them agreed it was worth the tradeoff.

The torqs caught their scent by the second night of travel. As the sun set, a trumpeting far in the distance announced a torq beginning its hunt. Soon, more joined in. They weren't close, but there were a lot of them.

From that moment, there was no sleep for anyone. Sadavir pushed them hard. They traveled through the night. At regular intervals, Sadavir had people making false trails and distractions. The younger, stronger ones ran ahead down fake trails, backtracking to rejoin the group, winded and puffing.

Others crafted holes in the ground or in trees that could hold a torq off for a time while it tried to get inside. For bait, they used their own blood. Everyone took a turn. When Sadavir told them to bleed, they bled.

Fear, exhaustion, and Sadavir's own dark manner pushed them into meek compliance. They only got to rest on the occasions when they needed to make a new distraction trap. They sat around, chewing on dried meat while two green Stone holders crafted a living wooden cage in the trunk of a massive tree. Later, Sadavir would choose one of them to cut himself or herself so that they could add a wad of bloodied cloth to the center of the cage.

"Vova said you survived one of these things." The older woman sitting by Sadavir said it as a statement, but he could hear it for the question it was. Could he defend them against one of the creatures if it caught up with them?

"That's not exactly how I'd describe it," he answered. "One of them attacked me in the night. I was wounded and managed to use my bloody clothes
152

as distractions to run away until Vova and his team rescued me. There's no surviving the torqs."

"Torqs?" she asked. Sadavir thought her name might have been Vala, or something similar, but he didn't feel like asking. She was one of the oldest people to have come up to the highlands. Her hair was a dirty gray and wrinkles lined her face, but she was as tough as old leather. She had been one of the few who had never faltered or grumbled in all of their mad dash back to the scaffolding.

"That's what Vova called them," Sadavir offered. "He said they were some sort of demon from your myths."

"I'd say his interpretation is a little flawed," she started. She continued to explain as Sadavir looked irritated at the backhanded slight of his dead friend. "Vova was a great man and we all owe him our lives, but he wasn't exactly a scholar.

"The torqs of myth weren't demons, they were gods that ruled before the time of men. They were the physical manifestations of the wrath of nature. Lightning, earthquakes, storms, that sort of thing. Anything that tried to establish order, or create something more than what nature provided, the torqs would destroy."

"I could see how ancient people might make that connection with these things," Sadavir commented. "What happened to them? In the myths, I mean."

"The same thing that always happens." She paused and spat, barely missing his foot, an old woman who was past caring about the judgments of others. "Greater forces arose to oppose them. The gods of men banished the torqs from the world of men. It's said that they were locked in a purgatory where they would constantly eat each other, but be reborn before they were ever completely consumed."

"Who were the gods of men?" Most Creators worshipped ancestor spirits, though few were truly devout. The Destroyers had a complex religion that Sadavir still didn't fully understand. It had a lot to do with justice and a complicated afterlife that sorted out the injustices, but Sadavir had never heard about any "gods of men."

"Ancient superstitions, I imagine. Most of the old myths end with some mighty hero or kind god showing up and saving the day when the people were too weak or stupid to save themselves. Give it a couple hundred years and you'll be a story just like them, boy. People will talk about the young god or demigod who shook the people out of their own dumb notions."

"I'm no god," Sadavir said with more bitterness than he intended. "A god could have saved his friend."

"I don't think those gods and heroes back in myth were any more godly than we are. Likely they were just folk trying to survive.

"As for their powers, the only person ever had real power that was reliably recorded was Amel."

"The man who changed us, right? The one that started the Stones."

"That's right. And you'll notice that for all his power, the effort killed him. No gods, just folk, you see?"

"You may be right." A new idea had occurred to Sadavir and he spoke it out loud before he had thought it through.

"What if they were all Amel?"

"How do you mean, boy?"

"I mean all these stories of gods and demons and such. What if they were all Amel. A man that powerful could have lived as long as he wanted, couldn't he? Maybe he was around a lot longer than anyone knew."

"I suppose it's possible, but what difference does it make?"

"Not much, perhaps, but think about what we've seen, the beasts up here and the incredible cliff that keeps them away from us. I've never thought much about it, no one has, but think about it now. What if Amel had split the land, creating the highlands?

"That would have kept the torqs away from people. Then all he would have had to do was kill however many were left in the lowlands and he'd have a new, safe homeland for his people. They could finally stop skulking and cowering in caves like mice."

155

Vala, if that was her name, nodded over the idea. "It would fit his patterns. It was never enough to merely save people. Amel would always try to change the world itself, so that things would be better permanently. He never called down rain when he could create a well or redirect a river. Changing the people so they'd be born with Stones was just the last in a long string of such projects.

"We've never connected Amel with the cliffs, but after seeing these things up here and seeing how they can move and climb, it does strain coincidence that our land is sealed off from theirs by a barrier that seems custom built to keep them out."

"And we messed with it." Sadavir's voice was low, barely above a whisper. "We changed Amel's plan and now..."

"Weren't you listening?" she interrupted him. She was the only one who wasn't fully intimidated by him at this point. "He wasn't some god with a plan of infinite wisdom. He was a man with incredible power, that's it."

"If that's true, then he should have killed them." Sadavir's eyes grew even darker as his mind explored the possibility. "He had the power. Why split the land? He should have hunted every last one."

She raised an eyebrow at him. "Would you do it, boy? Would you kill them all? That's an awful lot of killing."

Sadavir clenched his teeth and his chest shook

156

as he drew his next breath.

"Yes." he whispered fervently. "I would destroy..."

Everyone in camp jumped, startled, at a new bellow from the night. It wasn't much closer than the others, but the volume and tone were so much more than anything they'd heard before.

"What was that?" asked a nearby man.

"An alpha," Sadavir supplied the answer, staring off into the distance as if he could see through the trees. "But a larger alpha than anything we've seen so far. That herd we passed had hundreds of these animals in it. An alpha that could hold together a group of that size would be something more than a monster."

He looked down at the old woman he'd been talking to, though he didn't remember standing.

"I dare say anyone who saw that would be forgiven for thinking it was a dark god."

# Chapter 23

Sadavir didn't have to issue a single command. Everyone sprang to their feet energetically, as if they had just had a good night's sleep and a hearty breakfast.

They had been afraid before, but that bellow had brought a new flavor of tension to the evening. Urgency marked every motion. They were now bordering on panic. Sadavir used that panic to drive them through the last stretch of their journey.

When the tired, thirsty, and bloody crew finally broke through the trees the next morning, clinging to one another for support, they saw the watchtower Aric had made. Sure enough, Aric was on it and waved to them, already starting to scramble back down the tower. The others joyfully started to rush forward, though a few stopped and watched Sadavir, who had pulled a knife from his belt.

They had stopped asking him questions, so they only watched solemnly as he drew the knife across the back of his forearm, opening a cut that dripped blood steadily. Sadavir then walked the tree line, swiping blood from his arm as an artist dabs paint from a palette. He dabbed each tree with a spot of blood as he came to it, as if marking his territory. He marked over forty trees in this way, covering a swath of the tree line nearly a hundred yards long before wrapping his arm tightly in a ripped portion of his shirt.

When he finally rejoined the main group, they all quieted at his approach. Aric rushed forward to greet his son, but pulled up short as their eyes met. There was no joy in Sadavir at seeing his father, no relief at having made it back alive. They were hard eyes.

"We have to destroy the scaffolding." Sadavir got right to business. Aric nodded.

"They were explaining it to me. We didn't know they could climb so well."

"We never thought! All of our best and brightest and none of us saw the danger," snapped Sadavir. Aric breathed in deeply, eyes narrowing, but Sadavir matched him stare for stare. "All we can hope is that we're not too late."

He turned away from Aric and started commanding the others.

"I need workers in both metal and stone. Everyone else can start heading down, help the wounded."

They shuffled a bit as they obeyed his orders.

"Aric," Sadavir addressed his father and the burly man cocked his head at the formal tone. "We don't have enough metal workers up here. Nobody had planned on finding much metal up here. I need you to head up the crew dismantling the scaffolding. It might not be enough to have the scaffolding down, we need the cliff face itself repaired so these things don't have anything to hold onto."

"You can't..." Aric started to object. Sadavir cut him off.

"Just listen." It wasn't the volume of Sadavir's voice that sliced through Aric's arguments, it was the emotion behind it. It was impatient and angry, emotions that Aric had never heard from his son. They had been through so much together, but even in his darkest moments, Sadavir had never shown his father anything but the deepest respect. The lack of it now shocked him.

"Some of these things would have incredible reach if fully extended. I also don't think we've seen the biggest of them yet. I think we'll need a good forty yards deconstructed before we can consider it truly safe. I'll stay here and guard until you call out that you've made it at least that far."

"But..." Aric started again. This time, Sadavir stopped him with only a raised hand.

"We'll tie a rope to the tower and I can climb down that once it's clear. I don't think they'll show up before we're done, but if they do and they start climbing down on top of us, we'll have doomed our entire land."

Aric's vast shoulders sagged, half from the changes he saw in his son, and half from the knowledge that Sadavir was right. There was too much at stake, but Aric still hesitated to offer his son to the mercy of the monsters that ruled these highlands.

"I will need one more thing from you before you go, however," Sadavir finished. He held up his armbands. "I'm going to need something a little more aggressive."

*******

Aric had been muttering and shaking his head throughout the entire experience. In spite of his unintelligible protests, he worked quickly and efficiently, no wasted motions. He had recruited one of the few remaining Destroyers with a dark blue Stone like his own and even now, a pulsing blue light rippled from Aric's hand into a metal strut that had been pulled from the defensive spikes around the base of the tower.

The metal seemed to flow under the light, like a puddle of water would flow under the force of a strong wind. Sadavir thought he could see ripples along the surface of the metal as it shaped under the power of the Stones and the combined will of their masters.

Even in his dark mental state, Sadavir knew

better than to try to rush his father. If it had been a simple metal spike, that would have happened in under a minute. But Aric was still, at his very core, a blacksmith. The brittle nature of crafted metal offended him on a basic level. For all of their experimentation, they had never been able to make steel crafted by the Stones half as durable as steel that had been truly worked in a forge.

So now he compensated for the lack of resilience with a more advanced design. In spite of himself, Sadavir found himself staring in wonder, much as he had as a boy, as his father shaped the metal. He knew it was the Stones doing the work, but one wouldn't be able to tell that from the intensity of Aric's gaze and the sweat beading on his brow and running freely down his face.

A long, sharp blade, like a sword, extended the full length of Aric's arm. There, the similarity to a sword ended. There was no handle at the bottom. Rather, an oblong piece of metal with hooks at both ends opened with a hinge.

The sharp part of the blade was thin, barely thicker than a butter knife. It was reinforced in the back by an intricate web of small steel rods that twisted out of it like roots. The tangle formed a fascinating pattern that formed back into a solid piece of metal, all in a space no wider than three of Sadavir's fingers.

"Why not make it a solid piece?" Sadavir

couldn't restrain his curiosity any longer. "Wouldn't that be stronger?"

"Thicker doesn't always mean stronger, boy," Aric snapped, absorbed in his work and his thoughts. Still, he continued to explain. "This will be lighter without all the extra steel. You'll need speed more than crushing force anyway. Besides, this allows me to align the lines of tension against the point of impact. Even a small twig can stab your hand if you jab it in directly. I'm doing the same thing here, but with a hundred points reinforcing a single edge."

Aric held the finished product up to the light for inspection. To Sadavir's eyes, it still looked frail, but he would grow old and die before he second-guessed Aric's metalworking. Aric grunted in satisfaction and placed it next to its exact twin he had already completed. Then he leaned down and picked up a suitable rock.

He continued his instruction as he ran the rock in smooth motions down the blade of one of the slim weapons. Crafting also failed to create a truly sharp edge. That still had to be done by hand. For several minutes, the rhythmic grind of stone on metal was the only sound. Finally, when he deemed the edge sufficient, he spoke again.

"If you do have to fight with these things, make sure you make every hit dead on. These are only strong in one direction. A heavy hit on one of the sides would likely snap it. Come on then, give me your arm."

Sadavir moved to obey, but stopped as a sound washed over the barren ledge. Sadavir knew it all too well. It was the roar of a torq that had caught scent of its prey. Every face turned to the sound and every heart skipped a beat.

Watching his father work the metal had started to soften Sadavir's heart. Now, that single sound penetrated his soul and turned it as cold and hard as the steel he wore.

"Quick!" Aric reached out and grabbed Sadavir's arm. For his part, Sadavir had never felt calmer. Ice ran in his veins and each beat of his heart was only another stroke against the war drum.

Aric paused in attaching the new weapon to Sadavir's armband. The symbol for Honor faced up. Aric started to twist the armband to an open spot. Sadavir stopped him.

"No. Cover them. Honor and love have nothing to do with what comes next."

"Sa…" Aric began, but emotions choked him. He swabbed tears from his eyes with a hairy arm and nodded, more broken in that moment than he had ever been.

"All right." He still nodded, though the motion was mechanical, as if his head were bobbing on a hinge. "If that's what it will take to get you home, son. But you come home."

A small and distant corner of Sadavir's mind

164

wondered why his father had become so emotional.

He couldn't see his own eyes.

As Aric looked up into his only child's eyes, he saw dark ripples course over them, mirrors of the ripples that seemed to press against the surface of the Stone dangling from his neck. In that moment, he saw that his son had become something Aric had spent his whole life denying.

Sadavir was a Destroyer.

# Chapter 24

Most of the remaining members of the party had already begun their descent down the massive scaffolding. Only a few had stayed behind to help Aric. There was the one who had been helping him with the metal sculpting. He was a young, fierce-eyed man named Dima.

Much of the crucial work would fall on Dima. It would be his job to deconstruct the scaffolding as the party climbed down. There were also two sets of light blue Stone wielders. They would smooth out the rock face of the cliff as the scaffolding was pulled out, creating a smooth surface that no torq would be able to climb.

Now, with the roar of the alpha torq, all the remaining people started climbing onto the scaffolding for their terrifying and slow climb down. Sadavir made it clear to them one last time that there could be no shortcuts, no hurrying, and absolutely nothing left behind that could give the torqs a path down to the lowlands. Anything less than perfect would be considered nothing less than treason and treated as such. Even with the crashing approach of the torqs, most of the men and women still had the good sense to be even more afraid of Sadavir.

Aric took one last moment to check the rope tied to the tower before lowering himself onto the scaffolding, which had already started to pull away from the cliff face under a rich blue light. It looked like it was melting away, like icicles next to a fire.

Their heads disappeared below the cliff, but Sadavir didn't see them go. All of his legendary focus was on the trees, which shook for only a second before the massive alpha torq burst through into the cliffside clearing.

Sadavir's emotions flicked from one to another in less than a second. At the first moment of reveal, his knees felt weak and watery. He immediately felt ashamed of his fear, a tear leaping unbidden to his eye. That shame turned directly to anger. A calloused hand brushed the tear away with unnecessary harshness. The eyes narrowed and his heart beat against his chest like the thunder of a stampede.

This last feeling he felt first in the back of his throat. It was a bitter, sour flavor that curled his lips and put fire in his gut. It was a feeling he hadn't known before, one his father and sweet mother had protected him from his whole life.

It was hatred.

The torq sighted him and let out a roar of excitement. Its hunt was at an end and a feast of blood and flesh was at hand.

Sadavir, eaten from the inside by an overwhelming desire to destroy, to kill, roared back. It came out like a tortured scream, ripping at his throat with the force of it. It wasn't deep or impressive, but those on the cliff who heard it shivered and paused in their work.

The warrior was unaware of the other torqs that had filtered meekly into the gaps among the trees. They had also been drawn by the scent of blood, but their fear of the alpha kept them in check. They would wait and watch. Perhaps there would be an opportunity to steal a morsel when the alpha was done.

The alpha approached eagerly, though still walking. His prey wasn't running, so there was no need to chase.

Sadavir waited and watched through bloodshot eyes as the creature drew closer. All of his attention was focused on the torq. He couldn't see the roiling darkness on his Stone, or see the ribbons of darkness that twisted and writhed across the surface of his own eyes.

The torq drew up when close and reached out with one of its unnaturally long arms. The claws on the end of each of the three fingers were longer than any sword Sadavir had ever seen. He waited until the claws were closing around him before he dropped below them, ducking into a crouch before leaping up under the hand, driving the spike on his armband though the creature's enormous paw.

He drove hard with his left arm, his feet below him pushing like he was going to jump, channeling all the power into the thrust. The blade sunk in and hit bone.

The creature had been moving so slowly and ponderously up to this point that Sadavir was completely unprepared for the quickness of its response.

The hand snapped away so quickly that Sadavir had no time to respond. The torq moved the hand at an angle, and the blade caught and snapped. It was a light thing for the torq, it likely didn't even feel the extra pressure it took to snap the blade.

For Sadavir, it was a crushing force. As the blade was ripped away, it tried to take Sadavir's arm with it. While it seemed like the blade snapped instantly, it was still strong enough to last a full half of a second.

That was more than long enough to lever the armband against the radial bone in Sadavir's arm, breaking it. It was more than long enough to jerk Sadavir from his feet, wrenching the muscles and tendons in his arm as the rest of his body was thrown like a discarded rag.

Sadavir hit hard, but still managed to roll into it enough to save his breath from being knocked out completely. He tried to push himself off the ground and was infuriated to find that his left arm refused to act. In the wave of shock and adrenaline, Sadavir couldn't feel much of the pain, but the arm hung strangely and trying to move it only resulted in bizarre twitching underneath the skin, as if the muscles couldn't contract as they once had.

The torq was licking at its injured palm, looking toward the other torqs that ringed the vast clearing. It made sense to whatever was left of Sadavir's logical mind. It was likely that this hulking alpha had only ever been hurt in fights with other torqs. When its paw was damaged, it would be quicker to believe a surprise attack from one of its own than to believe that a skinny lump of meat like Sadavir had somehow injured it.

Sadavir never took his eyes from the torq and a low growl rumbled deep in his chest like a wolf about to spring. He shrugged his right arm out of its tattered sleeve, then wrapped the extra cloth around the front, ultimately tucking it in the back of his belt, creating a crude wrap to hold his left arm to his body.

When it was still too loose, Sadavir reached over with his right hand, grabbed his left wrist, and pulled hard on the arm, cramming the hand into the belt as well. A corner of his mind screamed at the pain and the extra damage he was doing to his body, but Sadavir didn't care.

All of the shame, fear, guilt, and loss he had felt over the last month had now distilled inside him. He would destroy this thing, this beast that had taken so much from him. In his fevered mind, this torq in front of him had injured him, killed his friends, killed Vova, and would now kill him.

Sadavir had already accepted his death. He wasn't listening for his father to call out that it was safe to climb down the rope. Even if the call came, he wasn't leaving. He had accepted that battle with these nightmares would end in his own death. All that he asked, all he prayed from whatever fate, gods, or spirits that might exist, was that he could live long enough to kill his own murderer.

No, rescue and escape had no place in Sadavir's mind. He didn't believe in them. He didn't want them. He wanted blood and dominance, and he wanted it so badly that his mind and body quivered, hungering to stab, rip, and pound at his enemy until the darkness took him.

So he ran at the alpha, an explosive sprint to catch it while it was busy glaring suspiciously at its thronging herd.

Sadavir caught the thing still crouching. He couldn't reach the head, where he most wanted to strike, but he got as high as he could. He jumped and managed to plant one foot on the bent calf of the massive creature, using it as a platform to leap higher. His timing was perfect, his balance flawless, and he hit the back of the torq's thigh with his blade extended and the weight and motion of his body perfectly aligned behind it.

The blade sunk deep and Sadavir wrenched it free immediately, not intending to lose his remaining weapon.

The alpha trumpeted in pain, thrashing away. Sadavir evaded the motions easily, almost contemptuously. He exulted in the pain of his enemy, reveled in the piercing vibrations of the anguished bellow. Blood ran down the blade, over his hand, and dripped to the ground. He wanted more.

He set his feet for another charge, but he didn't get the chance. The torq whipped around to face him. The confusion was gone, it was clear that this small creature was what had harmed him. Now it roared battle and charged at Sadavir. It was crouched low, leaping in low bounds.

Even after all his experiences, Sadavir wasn't ready for the speed of the creature. There wouldn't be time or space to dodge. The long arms and wicked claws were sweeping together like a child catching a fly. In the center, roaring fangs gaped open like a spiked cave.

In some sane, forgotten corner of his mind, Sadavir flashed back to his childhood, when his father would train him by ambushing him in his own home. One time, his father had come low and fast, just like this monster. Once more, Sadavir's training reached forward to guide his actions.

He jumped.

# Chapter 25

Of course, with the size of the alpha torq, there was no chance in clearing it entirely, like he had his father so many years ago. His plan was to leap high and to the left, aiming for the upper arm that would be moving a little slower. He could then use that as his next step, leaping from the arm onto the back or head, where he could deal out some significant damage.

However, even enhanced reflexes and a burning killer instinct don't make crazy plans any more plausible.

Surprisingly, his initial leap did indeed get him to the upper arm of the torq, though it was more a function of the arm moving faster than expected than Sadavir having leapt far enough. Once there, his foot slipped on the soft, thin fur and went out from beneath him, shooting forward. His back bounced off the arm a single time before the sweeping arm was gone from beneath him and Sadavir fell the remaining distance to the ground back first, hitting flat and hard. His breath left him in a single gasping rush.

He rolled to the side. He couldn't breathe yet, and couldn't effectively spring back to his feet, but he knew he couldn't hold still. A moment's rest would certainly end with him impaled on a massive claw.

The thrashing jarred his left arm free of its makeshift sling. The shock of the initial injury was fading quickly and his cheek twitched against the pain.

As he pushed himself up with his right arm, his eyes locked on the alpha. Its initial rush had been swift and powerful, then it had tried to reverse directions quickly when Sadavir had dodged. The vast momentum of the creature, combined with the worn stone floor here at the edge of the cliff, caused the torq to lose its footing and it slipped, sliding toward the edge of the cliff.

Sadavir was already pushing himself to his feet with his right arm. The left still hung useless, bones and sinews alike broken and torn. He struggled to draw sips of air into his burning lungs. Still, for all these injuries and obstacles, he couldn't dare waste this chance.

An enemy's mistake is a rare and precious gift.

The massive creature was struggling to get up. As he shambled closer, Sadavir could see why. One of the alpha's arms had become caught in the structure of the tower. Distracted, it now thrashed and jerked against this annoying impediment.

The tower bent and folded as if it were no more

than a collection of green woven sticks. Loud snapping and groaning sounds announced the separation of the tower from its anchors in the stone. The other massive arm pawed at it until the other arm was free. The pushing motion sent the tower over the edge of the cliff. If Sadavir had been watching, if he had been in his right mind, then he might have noted the loss of the rope, might have felt some alarm at this final death knell to his chances of returning home.

As it was, Sadavir didn't spare a glance for the tower. His entire attention was on the leg nearest him. While the torq was disentangling itself from the tower, its lower half had remained sprawled, the legs largely motionless.

Even as the tower dropped away into the vast nothingness, Sadavir was swinging his arm in a wide arc. He had used the blades for stabbing thus far, and they had penetrated easily. This was the first time he had used the cutting edge and he wanted it to be perfect. So he brought it down hard, but in a smooth arc, so that the blade would immediately be drawn across the flesh, rather than slamming into it like a hammer.

It was not a move he had tried before, having had no training in sharp weapons beyond blocking them. However, his black Stone was a writhing mass of tangled dark lines on his chest and the darkness was reflected in his own eyes. Like never before,

Sadavir was truly in tune with his Stone and his purpose. He was destruction. He was death. He was the violent end to all things. No amount of training could have matched the perfect killing instinct that now pulsed in his fibers.

So the cut was perfect, the angle sublime, and the damage devastating.

The alpha roared, this time in true pain and alarm, not just rage and surprise. Sadavir crowed in savage delight at the sight of the wound, deep and severe, the tendon above the ankle critically damaged.

His moment of gloating was his undoing. The torq snapped a backhanded strike at the source of his pain. Sadavir tried to jump out of the way, but a claw struck him full across the chest.

For the first time, Sadavir's armor of hate was cracked. The claw angled across his chest, hitting his dangling left arm first, breaking the bone under the bicep and carrying through to smash into his chest. It was a full body shock and Sadavir couldn't tell at first what had happened. But even as he flew through the air, hit the ground, and rolled, he was already hunching and gasping, trying to protect that side. Every nerve in his body screamed that things were now seriously wrong.

He was broken.

It will forever live as a testament to Sadavir's iron will that he rolled to his knees in that moment.

Any lesser person would have laid down and held their breath, fearing the sensations that would come the next time the chest moved.

Sadavir still breathed, and he could both feel and hear the grating of shattered ribs beneath the skin. Even covered by his shirt, his left side didn't look right. It had a caved and twisted look that testified of massive internal damage.

His right side, miraculously, was untouched, aside from the regular scrapes and bruises one would expect from a battle. He didn't bother using his right hand to probe his wounds. There was nothing that could be done anyway.

He felt an urge to cough rising sharply within him and he forced it down. He knew what he would see if he did.

The alpha was thrashing nearby. The legendary persistence of the torq had finally been broken. It no longer tried to find or attack him. It tried to rise over and over again, but the more it tried to use its injured leg, the more it pulled the wound open.

Sadavir remained on his knees and watched, all the while struggling to keep himself from coughing. The alpha's leg was ruined. Though it was a single cut low on its leg, it had been a killing blow. A creature that large would not be able to survive with one leg. Even if it somehow survived the wound itself, its rivals in the herd would finish it off easily.

Of course, such a gruesome scenario wasn't

actually likely. The amount of blood coming from the wound surprised Sadavir. It seemed as if the liquid were under intense pressure and now that it had an exit, was gushing freely.

The creature's movements were as vigorous and frantic as ever, but there was no hope for it. Constant blood loss was unsurvivable for any creature, no matter how strong. The bleeding had to be stopped or life would simply cease.

Sadavir's musings were brought home sharply as he lost the battle against his own body and he coughed violently. He didn't bother to cover his mouth and bright red blood colored the ground in front of him. His left lung was punctured. Sadavir didn't know if such a wound could stop its own bleeding, but from the amount of blood he had just coughed up onto the ground, it must have been a significant wound on the inside.

Olya had talked about such internal wounds. There was an herb that would stop the bleeding if it could be administered fast enough, a small fern with little white flowers. The knowledge made little difference to Sadavir. He hadn't seen any of the herb here on the heights and there was no chance of him wandering around to find some, much less boiling water to make a tea.

Even as the thought crossed his mind, he smiled through bloody teeth at how ridiculous it was. He wouldn't die of internal bleeding. Even serious cases still managed to hold on for an hour or two. He only had as long as it took for the other torqs to realize that the alpha wasn't a threat anymore. Then they would move in. They might kill him first or the alpha, but it wouldn't take long. Already the massive torq was starting to slow down.

As Sadavir knelt, breathing in short, shallow gasps and watching the alpha, the hate drained out of him, leaving him feeling hollow and emotionally raw. He felt a strange kinship to the massive nightmare beast. Now that it wasn't trying relentlessly to kill him, he could no longer picture it as a vengeful demon.

It was an animal, perfectly crafted for destruction and driven by its instincts. Just like Sadavir himself, he realized.

And now they would die together.

The idea formed a bizarre kinship with the beast in his mind. Each of them was an absolute, awe-inspiring pillars of passion and strength. They had met as equals and had killed each other. The only difference was that Sadavir knew he was dead. The torq hadn't quit trying.

It didn't seem right.

# Chapter 26

No, it wasn't right, it wasn't acceptable that his opponent should die weakened, ripped apart by its own kind now that he couldn't assert his dominance.

A new source of will surged to life within Sadavir. He would not wait to die and he wouldn't let the alpha suffer to death on the cold rock.

He would end it now. He would finish what he had started. He would kill the alpha, and probably finish himself off in the process. It was a better ending for them both than waiting for weaker creatures to take them.

He couldn't clench his left arm to his side to help support the ribs, that arm hadn't worked before and was even more wrecked now. He let it hang useless and pulled his right leg up underneath him, getting his foot on stone. His damaged core wouldn't allow him to lift his left foot, but he was able to set his foot solidly against a rock. Then he pressed hard with his right foot, using the force to twist his left foot into an upright position. He was on his feet.

The effort cost him and he coughed again, more bright blood washing down his chin and onto his chest.

Still, his legs and hips were undamaged, as was his right side. He could still move. He stepped cautiously toward the injured torq.

Luckily for Sadavir, it was closer now. It was ignoring him, but was using its massive arms to pull itself towards the tree line. Sadavir didn't know what instinct drove it that way. Maybe it felt vulnerable and wanted cover, or maybe it was more intelligent than he had thought and wanted to use the trees to help pull itself upright.

Sadavir staggered on a collision course with the creature. He didn't have much longer himself. There wouldn't be many places on a creature like this that would cause instant death. As it was crawling, the neck and eyes were largely off limits. And even having accepted his own demise, he wasn't in a hurry to walk right into the waiting claws of the creature.

No, it had to be the heart. For all their bulk, the creatures had oddly long torsos, not broad and bulky, so his blade might be long enough to reach through the ribs and get the heart. As overworked as it would be right now, even a small wound would be instantly fatal.

As with most things in life, the trick would be in the timing, and Sadavir was a master of timing. He would need to make his move right when the arm was fully extended, decreasing the likelihood of the alpha noticing and stopping him.

Under normal circumstances, it wouldn't even be an inconvenience for the man who could leap from tree branch to tree branch and block launched rocks without thinking. Now, however, Sadavir's body was unable to match what his mind commanded.

He was feeling lethargic and a little dizzy. He knew what was happening from his years of training. The reality was that the body only had so much blood. When the demand for blood in other parts of the body got too great, the body had ways of prioritizing. It would keep blood back from "non-essential" parts of the body to feed what was necessary. It was called shunting.

Sadavir hadn't been lifting heavy stones one after another, but he had lost blood internally. So his body was shunting blood now, trying to keep plenty around the heart, which left less for his brain and many of his muscles.

His mind felt fuzzy and his muscles were slow to respond. He would not be able to sprint over to the torq. Worst of all, he was on the wrong side. If the creature's anatomy was like a human's, the heart would be on the left. The torq's right side was facing him. Sadavir did not trust his ability to walk around the beast and catch up to it without tripping or getting hit by a random thrust of a leg.

He'd have to get on top of the thing. The effort would likely cost him even more internal blood loss, hastening his end, but it was the only way he knew to make it decisive.

His moment came and he hobbled into action. The arm was fully extended, gripping at a crack in the rock and pulling itself forward. Sadavir went up to the side of the creature and pressed his right side up against it, his hand reaching up and gripping a handful of the thin gray hair.

There was no reaction from the fading alpha. So Sadavir was dragged along with the beast for a moment until the arm was fully retracted again. That brought the arm close, almost close enough to crush Sadavir against the thing's torso. It was what he had been waiting for. He cocked a leg and pushed off the massive limb, pushing himself on top of the torq. He repositioned his grip to a higher location and pulled for all he was worth.

He screamed, or tried to, at the pain as his body stretched, dragged solidly up onto the huge creature by his right arm. His scream of pain was interrupted by another cough that mixed red with the gray fur.

But he had done it. He was now on top of the torq. The left arm was now extended and it was pulling again. Sadavir braced himself against the motion, though it wasn't too severe. He cursed his useless left arm again and used his right elbow to prop himself up and start to push himself along the narrow back to the other side.

Pushing himself to his knees cost him another scream and another cough, but he made it. He could even feel something like a heartbeat below him. It was slow and powerful. Sadavir placed the blade and lifted his right foot underneath him as he had before. There he paused, wondering if he could finish it without any further damage to his own body.

Ultimately he decided there wasn't any excuse to do it half way. He used the tripod technique to raise himself to both feet one last time. Then he locked his elbow into his side and let his knees buckle, using the full weight of his body to drive the blade home.

There was one moment of tension as the torq's muscles seized. Then, as fast as it had happened, it was finished. The muscles relaxed like a snuffed candle and Sadavir knew it was over.

He let his body relax, curving over the blade and the armband that had now effectively anchored his right hand to the torq. He didn't know if he could pull it free and he had no intention to try. The sun was warm on his back and the creature's fur was soft and warm beneath him. He coughed again and his blood mixed with that of the alpha's around the blade.

He felt oddly at peace. There had been so many mistakes, so many failures, but now it was over. He had rescued the survivors and had killed the greatest of the torqs. He could finally rest.

His head rested on the back of the torq, so his head was turned to the side and he was dimly aware of the herd that was beginning to inch their way clear of the tree line. They were still maintaining a respectfully slow pace, in case the alpha came off the ground suddenly, but their motion was consistently forward.

"Sadavir!"

"Sadavir!"

It was his father calling him, of course. Sadavir's drowsy mind recognized the voice and the concern behind it. The voice sounded hoarse, like Aric had been yelling for a while. Had he? Sadavir had no way of knowing. In battle, he became hyper-focused, often to the exclusion of everything else.

As his heartbeat calmed and everything went quiet, his father's voice returned to his consciousness. Sadavir smiled sadly. His father wasn't the type to ever give up, but he'd have to this time. As desperate as he would be to rescue his son, even Aric wouldn't risk this herd flooding down to the valley below. It would be the end of everything.

Sure enough, there was a long pause. His father had stopped yelling.

The other torqs were getting more bold now. Some were already close enough to sniff at the trail of blood that had formed after the initial wound. They would be on him soon. His eyelids drifted shut and he focused on the feeling of the warm sun. It would be better not to see it coming, he decided.

"Sadavir?"

# Chapter 27

His eyes shot open. His head cleared as heart-wrenching panic ripped him back to lucidity.

*No...*

He pushed with his mind against the reality, refusing to believe it.

*No...*

He tried to believe that he was hallucinating, a product of the blood loss.

*Please no...*

Strangely, the first overpowering emotion was shame. What he had done and what he had become to do it made him want to burrow his way into the rock itself, to hide from anyone who might see him. But here it was, and it wasn't just anyone:

It was Olya.

His mind raged against the possibility, a thousand reasons why it couldn't be true, but he knew in his very soul that he couldn't have mistaken that voice.

Somehow she was down there on the scaffolding with his father. Her voice hadn't been as loud as his father's hoarse cries, but it stabbed

Sadavir in the heart as truly as he had stabbed the alpha.

He filled his lungs as much as he could. Only the right one inflated as it should. The left made odd gurgling noises and again he was seized with the compulsion to cough. Instead, he channeled it into a single shouted syllable.

"GO!"

The shout was a pitiful thing, barely louder than he could speak normally. Blood dripped freely from his lips. He hoped that they would hear it and leave.

It had at least been loud enough to draw the attention of the gathering herd. Curious eyes turned from bloody patches and locked on him. They came slowly, but their motions were definite now. The alpha hadn't moved and the danger seemed less and less.

"SADAVIR!"

It was still hoarse, but his father's voice boomed once again. They must have heard his voice.

"CATCH!"

Sadavir turned his head to where the scaffolding had been, expecting to see a rope or something similar thrown up. It was a nice gesture, but useless. Sadavir couldn't catch anything, he certainly couldn't tie off a rope and climb down. The only comfort in it was that they weren't trying to come up after him. They wouldn't see him like this.

Then the familiar sound of a launcher twanged

and the sun sparkled off a speck of sky for a moment.

Sadavir's eyes struggled to follow the object, but couldn't. Then it landed and Sadavir knew why he hadn't been able to see it in the air. The object was too small, and it was completely clear.

It was Olya's Stone.

He stared in wonder for the space of a single shallow breath. Then he was writhing, trying to get some sort of leverage to pull against the blade, to pull free from the body of the torq.

He managed to get his right knee under him and started pulling frantically. The blade shifted slowly, an inch at a time. Meanwhile, his motion had attracted even more attention from the surrounding torqs, like a worm wriggling on a hook. They closed in faster.

Sadavir had the blade up less than half way when the first torq reached him and lashed out with wicked claws.

He threw himself to the side, the only move he was capable of with one knee as his only point of force. Something snapped and he rolled free, continuing to roll until he dropped off the side of the dead alpha.

One of the metal hooks that held the blade to the armband had failed. The blade remained above, sticking out of the alpha torq.

Then Sadavir was crawling madly, using both legs and an elbow to propel his broken body across the ground to where the tiny Stone twinkled in the sunlight. He was coughing uncontrollably now, blood creating a streaked path that he dragged himself over. The smell drove the torqs even more wild and they lunged and scrambled over the dead alpha, their fear of him forgotten in their mad rush for fresh prey.

They were too late.

Sadavir reached the Stone and scooped it up in a bloody fist. He rolled to his back to see the pouncing torqs as he raised the hand to his neck, where his own Stone lay on his chest.

Dark pure force lashed out from him and slammed into the torqs, flinging them back as if they weighed no more than rabbits. Their bodies hit ground broken and lifeless. The power surging through Sadavir gave him new strength and he rolled himself to his right, then up to his knees.

As expected, the rest of the herd was surging forward. They had no way to recognize or process this danger. All they could sense was the smell of fresh blood and the sight of a clear path to new prey. Sadavir worked the destructive power without any loud sound or intimidating flash of light. It wasn't showmanship, it was destruction in its purest form.

As they advanced, they died. Sadavir killed them from his knees.

He sobbed and coughed. Tears and mucous streamed through blood and dust as he whispered, begging them to stop.

He didn't hate the torqs any more. His hatred had died with the alpha. With each surge of killing energy, he felt like a murderer. He didn't want to kill them, but they wouldn't stop. *Why wouldn't they stop?* If he'd had the strength, he would have retched. But there was nothing else to do.

He wanted to live.

He wanted to see Olya again. He wanted a chance to come back from the darkness he had found within himself. He didn't know if redemption was possible, but he had to try and that required that he live.

So he killed.

He killed with thought and force of will. He killed everything that entered that desecrated clearing. When there was nothing more to kill, he didn't know if they had finally sensed something and stopped trying, of if he had massacred them all. He really didn't want to know which it was.

He knelt at the focus of a vast semi circle of death. He couldn't see how many were down, as his low vantage point meant that he couldn't see over the nearest corpses. Those that had fallen behind those nearest had merely dropped from view. But he knew they were dead. The unleashed power of the black Stone didn't wound, and it didn't leave survivors. Life was snatched from the broken bodies in an instant. It was likely that a creature killed with

190

the Stone didn't even feel itself hit the ground.

He turned from the field of the slain and started crawling towards the cliff edge. Luckily, he didn't have far to go. The angles involved meant that Aric would have had to fire the launcher nearly straight up. It had been a tremendous risk. Not that the Stone itself could have been broken or lost, it was tied to the person born with it. But if Sadavir hadn't been able to get to it, Olya would have lived the rest of her life feeling drawn to a place she couldn't go.

Sadavir finally reached the edge of the cliff and leaned out over the empty space.

Olya let out an involuntary cry at seeing him. Sadavir couldn't even imagine what his face might look like. He was only dimly aware of blood dripping from his face down to where they waited and watched. Sadavir locked eyes with his father, willing him to understand.

He lifted his right hand, holding Olya's clear Stone between two fingers. Even smeared in blood, it caught the light and glistened.

Sadavir stared hard at his father, nodded for a signal, then dropped the Stone.

If his lungs had been capable, Sadavir would have shouted for joy at the way his father patiently waited and then caught the Stone easily out of the air. He had understood immediately. It was possible that he had thought this through even before Sadavir had come up with the idea.

Then Sadavir pulled his own Stone over his head. It was added motion, but he lacked the strength to break the leather cord. He paused again, finding his father's eyes, then nodded again and dropped the Stone.

It was also caught easily and both Stones were passed to Olya, who also required no explanation or urging. Her hand raised and brilliant pure light wove around her, through her, then lanced out to find Sadavir.

Just as Sadavir could butcher and destroy from a distance, Olya's healing also worked at a distance, though not as dramatically. It was so much easier to destroy than to create.

Pain leaked away from Sadavir like water out of a sieve. His exhaustion only grew as his own body contributed energy to the healing. But feeling returned to the fingers of his left hand and the flow of blood from his mouth slowed, then stopped. His mind cleared and he had a moment to feel shocked at his survival.

Olya healed him until he was stable enough to stand and respond to them. Much more would have risked exhausting him so completely that he would have lost consciousness. He had no rush of adrenaline to keep him going now.

In the end, they managed to get a rope up to him, but he still lacked the ability to climb down. Instead, he looped it around a broken bit of steel that

192

was still anchored in the stone. He tied one end to himself and dropped the other end back to Aric and the others below. They drew the rope until it was tight, then Sadavir lowered himself over the edge of the cliff.

He tried to hold himself upright on the rope as they lowered him down, but soon a wave of weakness and dizziness made his hands slip and he rode the last ten yards or so dangling from his waist like a side of beef.

Strong arms grabbed at him and turned him so he could settle onto his feet. Light glowed again from Olya and Sadavir felt more strength returning to him, though it made him feel even more tired.

He still had enough energy to feel angry, however. He turned to face his father.

"How could you let a pregnant woman up here? I'm grateful to be alive, but that was reckless!"

Aric was completely unfazed.

"First of all, it wasn't my doing. Andre is the one to thank for that. Secondly, and most important, would you mind pointing out the pregnant woman in the group? I'm having trouble seeing one."

Sadavir was far too tired for wit and he stared blankly at his father. Then he turned dumbly to look for Olya. She was there, of course...

...but she wasn't pregnant.

"Wha...?" Sadavir didn't even know how to frame the question.

"We have a daughter, Sadavir," Olya beamed.

Sadavir was crying again, and hugging Olya as she held him in return. Larger arms encircled them both and the moment held for a long time.

"Not twins?" Sadavir asked when he could feel confident of his voice again. Olya shook her head.

"Not twins. I was that big because I was already full term. Our daughter was born big and healthy two months earlier than usual."

"Two months..." Sadavir started trying to put the numbers together and she helped him out.

"I went into labor very soon after you left, only a couple days after Aric and Andre had left to go after you. She's already a month old. Lauria is watching her."

"What's her name?"

"Dyesda."

"Dyesda," Sadavir repeated the name, smiling. "What does it mean?"

"Hope," Olya responded. "Do you like it? I worried about naming her without you, but everyone was saying what bad luck it was to have a baby without a name."

"I love it. Let's go see her."

# Chapter 28

The trip down the scaffolding and back to their village was grueling for Sadavir. He wanted so badly to hurry, but his body couldn't handle haste. They had to spend the time alternating between eating and napping to restore his energy, and healing him further. Never before had his body endured such punishment, so much damage. Even the pure power of the Stones couldn't restore everything at once.

Olya hovered over Sadavir and was always holding on to him, as if a strong breeze might blow him away. It rankled a little for him to have his wife see him so weakened. It also hurt him to see the fear and worry in her face. She had been a healer her whole life. Both of them knew that without the power of the Stones, his wounds would have been fatal. No amount of herbs or inner strength would have saved him.

He was completely healed by the time they reached the village, though, and he was able to walk normally the last distance to their home, held back only by Olya, who was thoroughly exhausted from the journey and the stress of Sadavir's rehabilitation.

Friendly faces and grateful waves greeted Sadavir, but no one tried to stop him to talk. Everyone respected that there was a more important meeting about to happen.

Lauria was already on her feet, sleeping baby in her arms, tears in her eyes, when the group came in. Sadavir crossed the room swiftly and hugged his mother first, careful of the baby. Then she coached him on how to hold his new daughter and he held her out tenderly, visibly afraid he might drop her.

A small, opaque, light blue Stone was held by thin netting that was pinned to the baby's clothes.

The awkward and uncomfortable hold woke the baby and she cried out. It was like a long, drawn-out squeak. Her high voice had a good pair of lungs behind it and she voiced her displeasure loudly, her arms and legs waving with random abandon.

Everyone stepped forward to comfort the new child, but Sadavir only smiled.

"She's ok, let me hear her a moment."

Baby Dyesda granted his wish vigorously, crying long and loud. Her face was beet red and her long cries were interrupted by little hiccups that shook her tiny body.

Sadavir sat there with a small smile on his face, soaking up the health, life, and vitality of his new child.

"She's perfect," he whispered.

*******

The next day Sadavir called the people together. It took a few days for the other villages to gather. Everyone came who was able. The stories had already made their rounds and had warped in the process. Sadavir was a hero all over again. The details were ignored or changed outright.

The only facts people cared about were that two parties had been lost in a land of monsters. Then Sadavir had gone alone and everyone had made it home again. Then Sadavir had saved all of them by holding off the torqs while the scaffolding was destroyed.

Voices that had joked about Sadavir being their king spoke seriously now. What more could he do to prove his worth? Who else could be a better leader than one who was both Creator and Destroyer? So all came to hear what he had to say. None expected what happened.

"I stayed behind because I wanted to kill a torq." he led off with confession. Many of the people didn't understand why he was so emotional about such a small thing. A few of the younger men even cheered the pronouncement, though nobody else joined in.

"While it is true that I didn't see any other way of saving the valley, you need to understand that saving people wasn't what drove me."

Anyone close to the stand from which Sadavir spoke could see the struggle as he begged people to see him. He was reliving fresh pain. Those far in the back would lose this nuance, having to read transcripts of the speech after the fact.

"When I had both Stones, Olya's and mine, I massacred those creatures so I could live. I don't regret my decision. I would make it again. I realize now what that means. It wouldn't have changed my mind if there had been a thousand more."

He paused, and seeing that people still didn't understand, he grit his teeth and made them understand.

"I would have made the same decision had they been people."

Eyes widened, a few hands raised to mouths to hide gasps, most looked like they were trying hard to not believe him. One of them even called out, though he couldn't see who it was.

"But you're a good man, Sadavir!"

Several other people shouted their agreement.

"Yes." Sadavir inhaled and exhaled fully twice over before he continued. "Yes, I am a good man. That's what my parents raised me to be. I have no excuse for what happened. So if a 'good man' like myself is capable of such things, I think we all are."

He gave them another few moments to let this new thought sink in. He wasn't only condemning himself, but everyone.

"I believe that any person put in my position up there would have tried to do the same thing. It was only the power of my Stone and the support of those who love me that let me survive where others would have died.

"When people feel threatened, they lash out. I grew up seeing that when people feared me. I didn't understand them then. I thought they were bullies and cowards. I understand them now, and I forgive them.

"Fear will twist any person, and the more power that person has, the greater the destruction will be when that fear takes over. I honestly thought that I was an exception. I thought I knew about fear, as I had seen so much of it in others. Now I know it lives in me. That makes me unworthy to lead you."

He said the last sentence as a pronouncement. It was what he had called them here to say. Another voice called out from the crowd.

"Then who is worthy, if not you?"

"No one is worthy to hold such power over people. Inevitably, someone will disagree with their decisions and want change. A leader will always feel threatened. We need to come up with a way of governing our peoples that doesn't place one person, family, or group in a position of absolute power. If you did that to me, then one day a great many of you would die at my hand and I would feel that I had only defended myself and my family."

"What did you have in mind?" another voice, this one very close, called out.

"I had it in my mind to let better minds figure it out." Sadavir smiled. "We have dozens of villages here, Creators and Destroyers. If this group can't figure out a better system of living, then you don't deserve one. But I believe you will."

More voices called out all at once, but Sadavir turned and started climbing down from the stand. One voice called out above the others.

"We won't let you down!"

The people cheered as one and Sadavir stared at them incredulously. He had shown them the darkness in him, had accused them of the same, and left them with no answers. Still they cheered him. He decided then that if his Uncle Amar ever came back, he would have a great many questions about how and why people thought the way they did.

For now, it was enough. The crowd was now discussing among themselves. Already, loud arguments were breaking out. It was a beginning, and a messy one, but they would figure out. Sadavir had meant what he had said. He believed in them, now more than he believed in himself. Everything would be all right.

# Epilogue

In the long days and short months that followed, a council of villages formed and decided on a rotating system of leaders. Andre was elected to be first, though he would only serve two years, then he would be forced to retire from the council and a new delegate from his village would be brought in. It was hoped that a constant stream of new delegates would prevent entrenched groups within the council from wielding too much influence.

Above the door of their new meeting hall, they placed what had come to be known as Sadavir's Creed: "Place No Faith In Power, Only People." The fact that Sadavir had never said it didn't seem to bother anyone.

Sadavir was able to fade from the public eye as people respected his desire to separate himself from the process. Still, people still gave him credit for the new government. Those closest to him expected him to argue the point, but his isolation was real. He had other matters on his mind besides who got credit for what.

Olya would sometimes find her husband looking to the north. Sometimes his jaw would clench, sometimes he'd make fists, and sometimes he put a hand up to his chest where it had been caved in. The one thing that was constant in all these episodes was the look in his eyes.

Olya could never quite describe the look adequately, though she tried several times when asking advice from Aric, Lauria, Andre, or Nadya. Every time she tried to use an emotion like rage, fear, guilt, or pain to describe the look, it felt wrong as soon as it left her mouth. It was all of those things and none of them.

Aric seemed to understand a little. He had been up there with Sadavir, had seen him before his battle with the demon beasts that ruled the heights. However, that proved little help. When she pressed him, Aric took on a haunted look of his own and couldn't be made to talk about it.

In the end, it was Nadya who offered the best advice. Her no-nonsense approach to life summed up the problem and the solution in a neat little package.

"Look, it's not healthy for men to have a lot of time to sit around and think. It gets them into trouble." She paused to glare meaningfully at Andre, who grinned sheepishly and turned back to his latest invention, a new law about land ownership. "Stop trying to understand something we're all better off not understanding and hand the boy a crying baby or something."

Olya took the words to heart and applied them literally. The next time Sadavir got silent and starting staring northward, she went and got Dyesda up from her nap. The little girl hated being woken up and started crying.

Olya marched her over to Sadavir and plopped her into his arms.

"Look after Dyesda while I go get her clean diaper rags off the line," she commanded curtly and walked off.

Sadavir looked down at the crying child now held against his chest. Instinctively, he started bobbing to comfort her. For her part, her arms were reaching around as she cried, a mark of her agitation. Her tiny hand found the top of his shirt and a bit of chest hair poking out. Her little fist grabbed it and pulled hard.

"Ow!" Sadavir yelped. Then he laughed at himself and the dark look faded away from his eyes like smoke.

Olya, watching from outside the open back door, heaved a sigh of relief. Sadavir wasn't all right. Not really. Not yet. But that didn't mean that they couldn't be happy while time healed what even the power of the Stones could not.

# About the Author

Lance Conrad lives in Utah, surrounded by loving and supportive family who are endlessly patient with his many eccentricities. His passion for writing comes from the belief that there are great lessons to be learned as we struggle with our favorite characters in fiction. He spends his time reading, writing, building lasers, and searching out new additions to his impressive collection of gourmet vinegars.

You can follow Lance online and on social media:
Facebook: www.facebook.com/LanceConradLit/
Twitter: @LanceConradlit
Instagram: @LanceConradlit
Website: lanceconradbooks.com

Or check out his Word of the Day series on YouTube.